TRAGEDY AND TRIUMPH

Mr. Teontry Waller

Tragedy and Triumph

Copyright © 2020 by Teontry Waller. All rights reserved.

No part of this publication may be reproduced, stored in a retrieval system or transmitted in any way by any means, electronic, mechanical, photocopy, recording or otherwise without the prior permission of the author except as provided by USA copyright law.

This novel is a work of fiction. Names, descriptions, entities, and incidents included in the story are products of the author's imagination. Any resemblance to actual persons, events, and entities is entirely coincidental.

The opinions expressed by the author are not necessarily those of URLink Print and Media.

1603 Capitol Ave., Suite 310 Cheyenne, Wyoming USA 82001
1-888-980-6523 | admin@urlinkpublishing.com

URLink Print and Media is committed to excellence in the publishing industry.

Book design copyright © 2020 by URLink Print and Media. All rights reserved.

Published in the United States of America
Library of Congress Control Number: 2020913200
ISBN 978-1-64753-433-2 (Paperback)
ISBN 978-1-64753-434-9 (Digital)
24.05.18

Grandmother raised me as well my loving mother since my dad was never in my life only when I was a baby If my dad saw me right now probably wouldn't recognize me at all. My dad is a deadbeat dad to me a different reason. He is the reason having mental health illness problem since being a baby I do look like my dad so what still don't care about him at all if he was real man took care of me but he didn't. I have been a real man since the age of 19 have to tech myself learn how to tie a tie also dealing with women on my own from past relationship been in some really bad relationships don't like breaking with people. I was happy in one relationship for a long time until everything change we stop seeing each other in person just really talking on the phone then told her wasn't happy anymore we broke up I thought special women guess not some women not loyal like Chris Brown these girls aren't loyal. There are some honest loyal women out there just have to find them at the right place and right time dating life can be very difficult at times past girlfriends had a lot family problem also person issue with their mom or dad some was very shy about opening up to me in the relationship for a lot of good reason. On June 7, 2015, was baptized at the hunter hills Baptist church for the time in my life!!!!! I start to accept Jesus Christ in my life about the age of 25 everyone went to church when they're younger always falling asleep in the church start going to church more in college a lot with a friend find a new church home always listening to the pastor at the church growing up in being a young kid. I am more of the geek growing in high school more geek in college was the Vice president of technology club also was working two jobs at that time I have responded more being a student first then work also being in meeting with them a lot. Well, talking to my program chair he told let the vice president position go cause failing in two classes I had one college professor teach me two different class in one term semester he told me you could do better on the research papers which got a tutor for that one class was critical thinking only class was hard to understand classes work and projects after the term was over went my school library to find out my grades high 80 average than another class pass with a 90 something. Pass both classes with no problem just have to stay focus on anything you complete in life also future you want to do never give up in life that you want to accomplish goals with your family and friend also in general born and raise from Atlanta Georgia peach state also am Grady baby. Childhood for me would be like about the same normal kid single mom in the house and grandmother support me having this mental disorders I was the very quiet kid growing up in the neighborhood a lot of people still know is the young boy. I been bullying before a lot of times in the neighborhood like pick on in the classroom people want to pick fights in hood grown up mostly in elementary school and middle school I had a lot of haters cause the clothes and wearing on me I think cause being short as well chunky with fat cheeks I had to learn to fight on my own time before being promoted to the 9th grade at Frederick Douglass high school in Atlanta Georgia. I went to turner middle school and F.L Stand then transfer to Walter White elementary school my favorite principal will always be Ms. Bolton she was way better than my old principal I also like Ms. Hamlet she was the assistant principal at Walter White unless never like being pick on at school all hated that shit wish they pick on somebody else my mom find out had a bully in the neighborhood she told me starting fighting back so I did. I always came home sore cut on my legs or forehead start getting more attention from girls in high school cause was taller than my mom now I was the very shy cool person in high school also got in a lot trouble in 9th grade didn't do none my work until have a very good conversation with grandma on the phone first. First time going out was nineteen went to the club drinking had fun on that enjoy the nightlife. Would say around the age of 21 start drinking really hard at house party and going with my best friend then start smoking weed a lot before we go out the club sometimes at friend party I had a lot of fun memory clubbing going to house party and just getting with friends to hang out after leaving the club is 19 years old throw up at friend house that next morning I had to clean up my throw up in the bathroom also first had a hangover was a very cool night for me. Of course my friends call me a party boy since graduation from high school in 2009 spending time with your best friend since you were young kids will forget about difficult things going in your so far start smoking weed hard ever since my grandmother died back in 2013 my mind then was like did not want any girlfriend at that point just want to get high like in the movie Friday you don't have a job it Friday just want to get high as a kite. But I was working at the time still in college really could focus at all my mom and I was going back to Atlanta cause had spoken to my program chair about school when people seen me back at school receive a lot of hugs didn't tell anyone had a family emergency all right knew going to have a long talk with technology program chair about grandmother and enrolled back in college. Very popular student at my college ever teacher that know me spoke with me. Program chair was very upset with me cause didn't call him back was in South Carolina I was crying a lot at the hospital seen my loving grandmother died in my face also my mother too I remember that day when she passed listening to music at the time something telling take my headphones out my ears so I did holding her hand until the doctors and nursery came in the room then try to bring her back to life they couldn't her heart stop beating it snow on that night. Every time wearing Nike blue sweater remember that she died still have flashback and anxiety attack start having anxiety attack also a year will wake up in the middle of the morning out of my sleep anxiety attack can happened at any time can't really walk straight at all have to your head until it go away my anxiety attack don't really be that bad going to house party have a clear mind just want to have fun enjoy time with best friend. I had to meet with the president of the college reenter school I was back in school won't start school until

March I had a few months get focus before classes start and working also had the pretty good conversation with the program chair. Just talk about finishing school life in general most important things that you have to let go it took very long time stop thinking my grandmother being passed away I didn't have a girlfriend at that time cause a lot of pain inside my heart and mind I just had to smoke it away took about a year release that pain and anger. The only reason why I attend college cause of my grandmother achieve successful thing that you can tell your kids one day so I finish college in December with the class of 2014 with an associate degree in information technology my mom was very proud of me graduated from college god dad best friend mom attend my college graduation I enjoy nightlife can't even count anymore being drunk having hangover after partying too hard. A lot of times women be choosing who they want to talk stop being so pick with men ladies I conversation with women at the club or club/bar some bee want to talk to me but everyone have different thing that women like on men ready to meet that special women that I know she the one for me then start a family and be married in a couple of years from now most of my relationship don't really last that long. I would say being in about two good relationship so far it was a couple women want a relationship with me told them no couldn't see it work at all. All of my best friends understand how feeling about anything Sydney Hudson is one of my best friends is one of my best friend that been knowing since college she a very good friend she can tell me anything going with she ask for advice on relationship life situation family men we talk about every day or every other day she very cool down to earth person she funny but she not funny then me I love her crazy self love all my best friends. The women I mostly like thick big beautiful women slim skinny smart fun funny short honest respectfully loyal faithfully be yourself cute who like video games also sports who want something in life that have goals like to have fun all the time I been thought a lot in life since being a baby don't like my dad at all if I see my dad ever in the future ask him what you want to do this to me we did not have any lights in the house for three whole months no gas to cook any food but god and pray I was bless with the money to get the lights and gas back on it was very cold he got pneumonia while we was in the cold I made by the grace of god. I thought that I was not going to survive being in the dark and cold house but God is faithful and true so I have in a struggle because I have been fighting for my disability check for three years I'm praying for a breakthrough in my clam god has bless me in so many ways thanks God I love God when I was younger spending time with my grandmother in South Carolina mostly in the summer. I start paying attention to her hair very different then most women my great-grandmother mom was India didn't know that until my moms say something to me about it. It very possibility half black half India from my great-grandmother genius cause a lot of people say feel like a warm heater my mom told that to me also women as well I decided to be a activists speak local elementary school and middle school my loving mother is going help with the public speaking about bipolar disorder and ADHA disorder seen being an adult very difficult with women telling this illness about me I will mostly explain to my future finance when the time is right to hope she accept about the ADHA disorder and bi-polar. One of my elementary teacher find out having also her daughter have it she told me one day in class I have a lot of one on one session with teachers explain different classroom assignments to be a good student start going to regular ed classes in 8th grade at Henry Turner middle school in Atlanta Georgia I had a favorite school bus driver was Ms. Jacksons in elementary school she was pretty cool with me I am pretty good cook in the kitchen learn from grandmother and best friend also learn from my mom how to cook. I knew a lot of teachers and students in school a lot people going to ask multiple question on ADHA disorder while doing public speaking I be prepare for all questions to help kids and adults also from parents that have children's with mental illness kids or adults it different way can trigger mental disorder would say about five ways really depends on how bad on the illness as for me it's couple way that can make talk different tone of voice in person or over the phone I try not to let people getting on my nervous so much as a adults. As a young kid it trigger very often like every other day sometimes every day of the week I have multiple hidden talents that keep explore new ideas to better myself in life would say listening to music while working out improve my fitness most of my family was not that different side of my family had some types of cancer do not want get cancer at all since being in high school start watching my weight being more health been a chunky kid grandmother feed a lot of good food gain some weight on me. I would say around 9th grade still little bit chunky then start losing weight on my own I play a lot of football in street in my neighborhood and tackle football I was always getting tackle playing football in the front yard and backyard my mom told me one day you start to be slim down she says not her fat chunky checks son anymore now my mom be calling sexy as well handsome every since having abs now. I might eat a lot of food still have a six-pack it took a long time get muscles and having a six-pack around the springtime and summer always lifting weight running playing basketball staying fit I stay fit year round do a lot of walking go to the gym I work on my whole body while working out mostly core legs upper body back shoulder work. Working out always clear my mind and playing basketball I play football in high school position that I play was Tight end/ wide receiver in my senior year of high school I run track as a senior it was the first time running track for me I play a lot of sports in the neighborhood never thought being on the football team and track team. I did run a lot in my hood growing up in like tag racing people of course play football too I want to play baseball in high school didn't make the team just play summer league baseball as a junior in high school I stay after school in weight room and playing basketball with my classmates that I knew in school everyone say I was good in basketball around the 9th grade should try out for the basketball team I know was going to make the team being in starting lineup probably be a shooting guard or point guard. I am still pretty good in basketball now always playing against my best friend Jeremy Joseph one day I will get someone to record me playing against my best friend in playing basketball we going to see who better then who on that day bring you're a game I play throw up and eaten up as kid always winning in that game. Playing sports was very good for development my skills in high school in future teach my kids how to play basketball football running track and baseball their choice to whatever sports they want to. I help them in and out of sports since my dad never show me how to play ball as a kid growing up I will guide my children's on sports and they have any question give a honest answer on the questions I will go to all my kids sports events to show support and any other events they want to do I just want to achieve successfully goals in the life for myself can't really know or tell if your children's have mental health illness until they have different behavior in school or at school if your children is very shy but not learning in school have a hard time focus on classroom assignments and projects I had difficult times focus on assignments and homework in school. Had a one on one with my grandmother with homework assignment and reading math problem until start doing the work on my own I did a lot reading program in the summertime and couple summer camp help to learn more thing about science human body healthy foods I was good science student and history-social studies it was slow process learning in the 1st grade got keep back in the first year of school didn't learn anything at first school at all. I had a lot of pretty good teachers in school learn from the best I had my first kiss in kindergarten it was good kiss I didn't get to any trouble in elementary school at all middle school was very popular in school no trouble in school until high school starting getting into some trouble with fighting walking the hall in 9th grade start going to class every day as a sophomore I was popular in school not that popular in high school I always hang with one of my best friend is Simeon Kemp then hangout with others friends as we'll. Start smoking black mild for a while in the background in high school start be lady man very quick I get that from my granddad in the family always keep a smile on all my females friends some on all my teachers first time smoking weed in middle school I didn't smoke like that in school at all until complete high school couple of my friends will have a get together at friend house for a party always having a good time out with friends enjoying nightlife. While in college have enough time to do community service events with several events eating healthy will make you be active walking working out and drinking right being in college was a good experience for me to see how college life really goes I want to have very own television show and radio station for my fans have celebrity guest on the show radio show anybody can call in ask question about me and special guest for that day. I will have different topics on the TV show and radio show if a person having problems with dating relationship give good advice for the situation going with them I was raised in a single parent house growing up as young boy seem my mom provide best way she could for me if she needs help with something grandmother will out too didn't have sister or brother at all wish that could happen grandmother spoil me all the time growing up being a spoilt brat for a while. Other people know me as a kid spoil me with different thing they gave me I am the only child could have a brother but my mom told she was pregnant before me she a abortion with her first kid didn't want to keep the baby mom keep telling she had death of pain with me while being pregnant for a while since being grown now I still having problems finding the right women to settled down with always finding the wrong women something going wrong in the relationship women been telling me have a baby face just know how to care of myself everyone that know me very cool lay back kind of guy also can be very funny anytime can be very helpful. as well with about anything brake a new brand heater that my grandmother bought my mom was watching me she thought was sleeping like baby but act like was sleeping then start playing with the heater while everyone sleep in the house then my grandmother find out about new heater she starts yelling at my mom grandmother told my mom watch his bad but she didn't watch good enough. Of course can be a flirt a lot with women see something that I like going to speak with her when I have a day that fans want to autograph session hugs and ask any personal questions they want to know about me just have a create mindset about new ideas about in life for a facts that writing a book about my life going is going to change my lifestyles meeting with different people about TV actors modeling jobs for me. You know how some people change from a normal person in life then be celebrity in life when I be a celebrity in life when I be a celebrity in life not going to change for anybody have to change my ways being married that all know body don't like a fake person or friend that not to be real with you at all sometimes the disorder can not want talk to anyone if you don't get enough sleep at all you will start getting mad for no reason one that can trigger mental illness. Sometimes mental illness will you go off on a person cause it don't make you think before you do it. It is a lot of people that have bad dose of it you will need strong herbs control your disorders mental illness if your parents drug you as a baby, not development your brain cells and your whole brain but if you eat vegetables blueberry drink herbs in your juice then brain will develop more having regular brain and mind just want to help people with mental illness and bipolar disorders having problem controls before they start different on you real quick in a second. Really don't know at all have a mental illness until my grandmother find out it and my mom I seen my mom being a few abuse relationships growing up as a teenager in high school been in a couple fight with her boyfriend's one time my had to hold me back because going to kick his ass or kill him on the phone with my mom cause was in South Carolina with my grandmother for the whole summer she was telling me that her boyfriend was hitting on her for a while. He was hitting her on her back really hard so I didn't get home until school starts in August still going on in the house he was only doing it not being home me and my mom set up a plan one day for him the plan went well-been control my mental illness for long times after being told about it long process know about the street life in my hood growing up being a young boy know everything about the street from top to the bottom. Always stay out of trouble did had some trouble in the neighborhood cause people want to fight me having a couple hater in school was mostly guys for different reasons didn't mess with my mind at all keep it moving forward in the books in life you choose your more passionate about doing in life grandmother raise me very well to be great man in life going to raise my own children's way better than my deadbeat father has seen a lot of people went to school with doing pretty good thing in life and some not. Pay attention in classes like normal students does was a little bit of class clown too people always joking in classes or the cafeteria sometimes after school before to football practice senior year was very good about the end of my junior year decide tryout for football make the team start training in summer with the team and coaches we had spring practice around march or April then put my focus on football mostly likely summer practice before start in the fall dealing with heat also sun learning the offense system new plays book training was June to July start running the hills footwork drills run with your position coach blocking drills for a week. Then the weights training and 7 on 7 drills before school start back in late august grind mode with running lift weight running routes catching passing I had the best hands on the team everyone knew even the coaches was telling me in pre game warm-up I play in a few games but didn't start at all want to be every down receiver and tight end of course people was ahead of me in that position now if I play quarterback have more playing time would the staring position in fall practice can throw a football in fall practice can throw a football pretty good still can and still play wide receiver play a lot of sports growing up as a kid keep me out of trouble too. Basketball was second love growing up mostly shoot the ball until start learning dribble better people have a very hard time guard me playing basketball around player on the court now play church league basketball for 2 or 3 years as small forward and shooting guard on the boy team play center hate that position not my playing style at all in pretty good shape senior year in high school playing football and running track when track season coming around little bit out of shape after the football season end thinking about tryout for the basketball team didn't have any basketball short with that day my body going thru a lot pain after football practice and track practice. I didn't not quite keep pushing my until cant anymore every time when I workout for couple of hours just lift weight running playing basketball have still have it playing football haven't touch a football since the 12th grade been a couple of years now since playing sports been active with workout lifting thing running errands playing basketball just like being fit eating healthy lifestyle will have longer life working out as well been on high protein diet since the summer keep me ground about different foods that not good for health and body. Going to try out different all natural diet food plans. For a little more tone and rip my frame body would mind helping people with health tips also fitness information and workout plans for better your health since being a fat chunky kid want to change eating habits and fitness goals in life for myself over the years from people say you look different now always getting attention from women am very friendly person who ever knows me everyone in life have fitness goals personal goals a goal they want to complete to feel very good about it. Different people have a lot thing want to complete before they leave this earth just want to be very good writer model actor television host radio station host and in the future be a great father also friend just a well round person that ready to leave the hood for good never want to go back at all so I was in my room sleeping hear them arranging while still sleep something tell me get up pick up my baseball bat in my room open the door catch him beating on my mom still my crazy self but swing at him about couples times until we start arranging in the living room for a long time. I say the next time you want to hit my mom again promise will going to jail today and I will kill you myself punk he all ready knew didn't like him at all we fight in the living room while my mom in her room then my mom say get off my son before she call the police he was on prorole for something he went to back jail or prison that day I was not that big in high school but a lot bigger since high school now I am lover not a fighter but if have to kick somebody butt. I never abuse a women before every in life grandmother told me never hit women that for punk I will play fight with women or my girlfriend if I have a girlfriend at that time my mom dad could pass for a white man great-grandmother her mom is India have some India white black in my family back in 2014 the lights out was off for about months there were cut back on in November by the grace of good living at local neighbor house for a while until we stay at friend house for one night. House was really cold after the lights got cut off few people know about this situation last winter living without your family to help you out when the times get at a point but is the other way around for me and my mom haven't meet everyone in my family so far love to meet the rest of my family it seems like my family get together when someone passed away in my family have good friends that give advice on any situation going with me difficult situation can deal on my own without advice also get second opinion just to make sure. Really don't tell my mom everything have to keep something to yourself haven't seen my mom happy in relationship in very long time since being younger very close with grandmother before she passed in 2013 before being baptisms this current year in the summer going thru a with hard struggle at that point for me I am in much better place with god hands right now in life been focus on great achievement that can have a better my finances very soon being a writing model actor television host own my radio station when I get my career of the ground my mom will be very proud of me and grandmother is looking from heaven too. Own mother say going to be better than my father in life it a few of ex-friends really don't understand about me they just care for their self about their plans to make them happy in life don't care them anymore beginning of the relationship with them did make me happy then everything else start changing about them really don't like breaking up with women in the relationship it suck too then giving a good reason to break up your ex-friend want to explain why they want a second change and mess up the first go round going to mess up again even worse. Moving forward with life goals new relationship then future plans get married having a family with a very special women just going to be a successful young smart man in life help people with bi-polar disorder and ADHA disorder explore the world with my friends and mom also do public speaking about mental health illness studying more research on mental illness can find illness without having surgery so it seems from my family background have black white India genius in the family sound cool with me going thru a lot of stress anxiety attack and depressing things going thru my mind after my grandmother died. As a adult seen the good and bad things happened to people and told me about speaking with kids adults parents about mental health guidelines healthy tips and tip control disorder that want sent to the mental hospital at some people will have to be able receive help on mental problems at the hospitals really don't know how mental hospital run on a daily basis for people that serious issue control your habits if you mental not stable enough. Albert Waller was born June 5, 1930 at Grady memorial hospital he had 6 kids and I stepson and got 7 grandchildren's three great grand children he went to with Dr Martin Luther king Jr he had all kinds of jobs he work at the Atlanta

Tragedy and Triumph

dairy as milk man and was a supervisor at Pepsi cola company he journey to work at funeral home as a personal assistant in bomb the dead and Atlanta paint place them after some time had pass his health fail he was sick with cancer in the stomach colon cancer he enjoyed women and drinking going to party he passed away at 55 years old on July 31, 1985. He white people in his family tree. He was the only child his brother and sister died at birth Margere Waller was born April 28, 1937 she is a native of South Carolina attend school there became a mother at 19 years and she leave Carolina came to Georgia to have a better life for her also her son he was born July 28, 1956 to Margere Burgess and gene Moore was his daddy she had varies jobs until she went to Atlanta area tech taking up dietary supervisor she graduate at the top of her class then she applied for a job at craw long hospital she work there for 33 years. Until she having health fail and she retired then receive disability check at the age of 57 she is a proud grandma of 4 grandchildren and 11 great grand children's she had 1 daughter her pride and joy she loved people she did not meet any strangers Leona Burgees was born on October 5, 1919 she had 5 sister and 4 brothers 2 grand Childers also have 11 great great grand kids 30 cousins I was born on January 6, 1969 in Williamsburg South Carolina I attend school at E.C. clement then J.F Kennedy west Fulton high school graduate on 1987 then on to trade school take up medical assistant for 1 years. Finally I became a can became a mother at the age of 21 continue on with being a nursing assistant until my health fail her being a mother of a son he was on May 9, 1990 I have been having a hard times these past 3 years know income to help to help mom myself my choices in life bad men and how they live and treat me live and be a better person and mother love god changing my ways of life and living spiritual life now in 2015 October 5, I am better because of god and living peaceful life keeping myself from the world now I am ready live a life be want god want me to live god fears life be strong spiritual be good life I got with my son and my future I husband. I need stability to live when I was a kid I put hair in my nose a button in my ear then I burn the garbage can to I like to play with fire my life has been alright until three years ago when I got sick help me lord Jesus I have neuropathy in my feet and arthritis in the ankle and pain my hip my son in his bipolar disorder is really taking a toll on me because he act like a kid most of time I love him with all my heart it is a lot stress on me because is a he selfish Teontry need herbs and some medication to help him stay come and continue to pray and believe my solid waste bill is do I need help paying it his father gave him medication to pleased his pleasure when he was smoking crack cocaine he tried to destroy this child. But god did not to see fit thank god my theory make me think that the white man want to destroy the black population I am a mother with love for my son and forgive daddy for getting high on drugs my son eat blueberry to stay balance he is god child he need to found his dad and have long talk my son has never found the right women to settle down with I wanted to take my own life and just give up on life but god had big dreams for his life to be model author writer business man actor he eat sub sandwiches from Kroger and Chinese food little bit of soul food squash broccoli cauliflower carrots pickles Doritos cashews I am good mother to him he never how to tied his shoes I get my nails done on special occasion my son I am so proud anxiety attack hard to deal without with my best friend like party to hard. Like a couple days in week time frame have to stay very still until wear off. Didn't know where they come from at all had to do some more research on anxiety attack while going out running errands a lot of time it does come at all only when at home me and mom been in few abuse relationship in the past time for a change have a lot best friends from day one still very good friends with still today still don't understand some women abuse there boyfriend for no reason at all most men cheat on their girlfriend a lot time never have a conversation with their mom or father how to treat men all my friends understand how be about with any situation relationships and women. Have a couple bad experience with financial trouble at point in my life support myself and helping my mother as well always keep myself ground living day by being a child of God teach me helping people giving homeless people money buy something to eat being started very talent with writing around the 12 grade doing school projects college work very much better for me at time really understand every writing projects and PowerPoint presentation first writing project was in August of 2014 about career goals short term goals and long time goals. All the writing projects papers mostly grades was A or B have a gift writing since my college days still help with a few people with writing project about any subjects have a side hustle with students in college understand apa format for a assignment few student willing to pay for me doing their work easy money for me can't complain about that all always willing to learn new thing in life about anything do a lot of reading on healthy articles and about sports injury reading also writing is a new hobby of my now for me listening to help me my mental disorders a lot every now then do some singing to growing up in a church a lot did a lot of singing being young a usher in a church before. Around middle school was in chores music teacher told me had pretty voice for a shy kid was his only student didn't talk about just focus on hitting different notes on songs for a grade he told me before graduate middle school in 2005 take your take singing have a good voice had problem rush with singing songs then he told would like to stay after class for the whole semester until being his best student then performance at concert in front of people was never also scary to sing with my classmates clam down after talking with my teacher told he was scary just told me take singing today say okay. I love beautiful big women since high school as a freshman year listening to music writing is a new hobby for me in life now something just don't want to talk about it with women at all until find the right women for me later in the future going to be married having Childers going to be living a different life for me listening to a lot r&b rap hip hop country pop some rock music and growing up in the 90's being in college always listening to music doing homework assignment some just sleep all day don't want to be both at all them when I look at my phone miss calls and text message from friends want talk about going out find something to wear that night enjoy night life very cool always doing fun things with best friends can't believe that I am mix with black white India in me going to the gym always clear my mind from a lot things happened with life just focus breaking a very good sweat playing basketball and lifting weights little bit of running. Living without a father in life really learn multiple things up in life last words grandmother told me in the hospital was be a good before she died in front of me seen my grandmother in the hospital bed haven't seen her couple of years first things she told me to arrive in the hospital was got big and all sit down for a couple minutes until she says come here holding her hands for a long time before going to settle in my grandmother house. As soon arrive at grandmother house had to clean up her house because it was dirty and nasty my mother brother is not the cleaning up type of men like me start vacuum the living room hallway as well the dinner room took the trash out from the kitchen was dishes for about 2 or 3 hours mom clean the bathroom her mom room for a hour or two hours after cleaning up the whole house with my mom just got a pillow some cover sleep for the floor was tried and sleepy then when the morning arrive woke up eat breakfast and watch TV then the house phone start ringing off the hook like crazy didn't tell my school had a family emergency at all. Came home from work and so my mom told me some bad news couldn't even take off my shoes then family members start came to visit the house for about 2 weeks straight family member also friends of the family giving food and drink talking to about different things going with my grandmother really didn't have a focused mindset for couple days very quiet people came to visit. Visit grandmother in the hospital every day until she passed away in front of own eyes since cousins aunts also since very good friend of mine while being at his house for the summer went bowling with my cousin just to get out of the house kitchen was full with drinks home cook food and plastic cup also plates spend time with younger cousin taking pictures talking about school with them did a lot cleaning up behind younger cousin they bad self also want to drink juice make a big mess in the dinner room food told them eat all their food before getting juice really enjoy time with my family for two long weeks before leaving back to Atlanta did a lot of eating food meeting new family members on grandmother of the family leaving the hospital after grandmother passed away that night. Getting in the car start thinking about to have a better lifestyle way better finances to buy nice for myself and mother really didn't talk to many people while in South Carolina was one of ex friend know about my grandmother passed very sad going back to Atlanta just listening to music create future plans about different things occupation want to do in life didn't speak any of my friends for about a few weeks until want to people went to best friend house down the street from my house just want to play video games watch movies all night long and morning. Took long time get back to my normal self then just want to party drinking and smoking weed just recently having a better feeling about life for great things helping with people mental health going have writing contest for high school and college students that don't have father in their life at all going to be a big brother for the winner grandmother did one on one advice being a men at early age of the house being a chunky kid growing up was cool at point in life start thinking about my future plans in high school did a lot of walking in the neighborhood walk from middle school didn't have any bus fare to get home if seen of old teachers that teach me from elementary middle high school still recognize me still look the same from high did tone my body more smarter since being in college for two whole year. Also have obsessive – compulsive disorder washing my hands a lot attention deficit hyperactivity disorder stand for ADHA mean can very hyperactive with childhood and being a adult just mild case of mental health illness growing with it have a hard time going to sleep some night it will take a few hours before until close my eyes day of the funeral start brushing my teeth use mouth wash getting dressed then couldn't think how to tie my tie somebody else tie my tie holding my little cousin at the funeral and the family car was sad at the funeral services some of the people was crying out there tears though the whole service at the everybody eat after the funeral just talk with different people in my family after the passed away in the family start thinking about way to help mom out. I prayed for him to come successful in this world me and my mother Margere did a great job with raising him in my being pregnant with this child he is the best thing that ever happen to me I got high pressure diabetes arthritis gout in my foot my life could be better if I had a income I am trust in god for a miracle this few weeks that is coming one of my boyfriend beat me so bad that my shoulders is severe damage from being heated bruise from this man I was living with in my house for about two years he was on crack cocaine he was a con man liar he did not know how to treat a women and my other abuse relationship this other man threat my life I thought I was going to die for real I got away from him he was a dangerous man to live with but I told myself know more crazy men or jealous men in my world. So now I am taking it slow and getting lesson from Steve Harvey about men thank god for Steve and his book on think like a man but act like a lady I am so proud of my son my three boyfriend was crazy he tried to kidnap me he very strange men he did not want me to come home to my mother from my dad died I was having hard time because he died we were very close then call the police came then I came home I was worry my mom. I turn to being bad girl because I lost my dad destruction was my friend for a while then I had a wake up intervention with older brother now he is on crack cocaine living with his mom on the south side of town my son is a trip he love to play a lot with his disease he act like a kid most of the time I hope and pray for a miracle so he will get better from his disease the life of being with a crack head for a husband and a daddy he don't not care about me and my son I have always love dark skin men but this one bad for me I went with a marry man twice the first lied about having a wife the second one she is a alcohol and he was ready for her to died I am getting all my advice from Steve and his talk show about man I been involve with guys in prison three or four time. One that was nice to me he was doing time for robbery a bank he got 20 years he got of prison 2014 in October and now there is one with no brain he smoke to much weed his mother suicide on October 7, 2015 he is really not got to depend on god for strength and guides and will for his before that I was talking to Demarcus a mom boy depend on his mother for money and he is grown man drinking beer and acting like a punk and little his mom treat him like he need a real women to tell to grown a grow some man hood and stop depending on his parents his dad was in jail he was a kid I am praying for a husband now in the next few years I want to be married to kind hearted and loving man. He needs to be a man with money or a good job and my favorite show is NCIS los Angeles and Washington D.C NCIS or NCIS New Orleans I am going to get me some money I don't have a man in my life right now my family don't love because they are uncared people I really miss my mom it flooded in South Carolina my brother got flooded in his and my cousin did I don't wish them harm is a challenge for me and have been working trying to not being a problem to my son getting money sealing make up shoes t-shirts make up brushes finger nails to people don't have a lot of money just enough to pay bills and get grocery for the house but me trust in god and believe in his word and staying strong god will see me through this storm of life. I am facing every day I love god and I know god love me I will always working hard and believe in Christ life can be hard sometimes Teontry be bless with his career and have a health and prosperous life and not suffer from not having education and knowledge and wisdom Romans 12-2 say that I can be anything my heart desire trust and believe in god you will make it all my life wanted to be my best at what I do and please my mother and god I still have a change to something good because of life will change I don't like being broke not having money. Always helping mom out with bills giving her money until she a income flowing start paying the bill in college for the first time ever since mom doesn't have any money yet am the only family she have right now until she meet more family members never seen before dating can be difficult at times for me barely communication with that person anymore really don't like hurting people feeling at all have to do what task. Always willing try new thing never did before at all in life seen mom been with couple of bad men's while in school she always can't never find the guy to married have too much going with their self have pretty good relationship in the past before being a bad boy around 19 years old and then now still a party boy going out with friends drinking smoking weed and going to party get together at friends house some people don't really see me a bad boy at all get my bad body genes from granddad have a lot good memory with grandmother being younger and being a adult now it was around September or October took pictures with my mom grandmother at the church growing up is Moriah Mount Church in Atlanta Georgia. It was fun taking pictures with my family that always will love until the day god send me to heaven that will be a long time from now wish had more time spending with my loving grandmother before she passed away in my face it is very good reason being a honest person and being real all the time grandmother told me stay honest with people good things will happened to your life and your career you have a passion for as long you have a good relationship with god when you ready for that point in your life last words she told before passed be good while visiting her in the hospital for two whole weeks had dark times at point at the age of 23 and 24 dealing with lost two different jobs didn't have a relationship god at all was nervous walking down the ally of the church join a church home. Mom was talking about this for a while until made the big decision walk when I am ready walking down the ally in May of 2015 coming home from church talking with mom for a couple of hours joining a church home now went to church as young boy like every Sunday or every other Sunday going to assist with my mom her soul food restaurant get her business start up very soon have a business idea of my own create technology company with a new style of technology for kids adults teenager grandmother will be proud of me writing a book about my life wish she was still living today. Just want to get myself as well my mom out the hood for good live a bright future with different career plans also will give back to all the schools attend give back to the homeless people start a charity company did hangout with the wrong people in high school didn't realize after the fact it happened going home from school one day got jump by some people went to high school with me still don't why got jump on that day at all guess there were jealous of me and they want me to join a gang in high school but did not join a gang at all. Didn't know it was a few people jealous of me while in school just wearing nice clothes and shoes too every day at school didn't say that much in class until high school start always keep it too myself have a lot of friends was very quiet and shy in school in the 12th grade was funny in science class always argue with couple of classmates stay after school a lot for extra credit work pulling up my grades not pass that one class learn from after school program in middle school and elementary school favorite speech teacher was Ms. Allen help with speaking more clear with my words and reading out loud had very hard time reading difficult words out loud in class teacher help out pronounce word to myself before reading a paragraph. Very shy to read out loud for a grade in English class did not like math at all in school need help with algebra and always have to study extra hard for math test grandmother help out with my homework and math class work math class did extra work help passing math class before the semester complete my mom been having hard time with money problem for about couple years before start going to college in 2012 of august she always getting on my nerves about money and food a lot while in college had three jobs gave her money buy her food if she don't want to cook on that day a lot of times she be telling things at the last minute while running errands for myself and mom have to get away for a night just be going all day out handle errands and going out with friends. Always want to have it her way because if she don't start getting mad about the situation got into a lot of fights in the neighborhood and at school coming home early from school got suspended for fighting want go back to school for couple days also got kick out of school coming to school getting late to class had to meet with some teacher about the progress with on school work and my grade's had a lot of favorite in school that help with me getting my social security check in elementary school learning experience was hard in the first grade until transfer another school social security stop my check around April or May of 2011. Always want to be a model since high school and want to be a actor very soon most of the jobs were technology and moving table and chair customer services was all right for a while until lost my job in April 1, 2015 first time working at a hotel it cool always a lot of walking for different tasks that need done before leaving working. Working at place call 200 Peachtree street really just cleaning plates washing dishes breaking down tables help out with the bartender liquor and ice also cups stay at that about 3 or 4 months didn't have enough days to work just work one day out the week made like 100 something dollars for 10 or 12 shift work over night ever time working overnight be very tried and sleepy just want to sleep all day being a night owl person like working over night cause not a morning person at all someday just want sleep if my phone ring just look at the phone roll over go back to sleep return phone calls also emails and text back people customer service job was a contract with best buy online order also in store order always staying up late listening to music and watching movies talking on the phone with friends. Texting playing video games with my best friend going out with friends didn't never talk to my father at all in life only my mom did dealing without a dad is all right learn things on my own time about women and how to deal with relationship start learning about sex until middle school had a sex education class very interesting talk about different sex disease for women and men didn't start having sex until 9th or 10th grade don't really think about sex all the time in general just focus on money food all the time having a better career in modeling be a actor and have number selling books want to be a writer have my own television show and radio station help out with my mom soul food restaurant start up for her business. Assist wither her restaurant if not out of town on business have passion for fashion since high school create a sunglasses clothes jewelry and cologne line for different styles for adults teens teenagers have been a go get for a in college enjoy doing volunteer work for any type event going on just been having create ideas for better financial buy nice things for me helping my mom out never thought about writing a book ever until now have a successful career in different ways going to be a very good celebrity with writing actor modeling as a business man own a clothing line Atlanta Georgia and maybe expand other states that looking for technology jobs want a television show helping people with dating advice looking for love cooking health business money gym diet plan and can ask any person tip help with their problem like the Steve Harvey talk show. Just like helping people for happy results more information that better outcome it is going to be very important for having a new accomplish complete in a new chapter in my life want to create a mentor program for teen's teenagers adults that don't have a father in their life at all and if there growing up in a foster home program will give away school supplies book bag notebook papers pens pencils 3 inches binder if there student Athlete pay for college visits don't have the money at all going to train in the off season before moving in their dorm room on campus give gift card to buy sports gear like basketball shorts socks running shoes under armor shirts give advice being developed into college star student athlete being in the spot light before enter their name in the draft give young people opportunity go to college for four years of college. That want have a good future while in college and after graduation from college this mentor program is for girls and boys between the age of 13-20 have to apply online give more details when the website has been create have just write a one page about haven't never a father figure in life since being a baby going to review to multiple candidate for the mentor program ever member going to receive a emails or phone call been pick starting the program very soon going to have a meeting with all member explain different experience you going to learn about life explore new things never did before every in their life time explain different reasons that you have to be a man or young women at early age since you don't anything about your father and never since your real parents. If they want to see their real mother or father have a few people helping find their parents still living willing to their children every kid should know about their parents also family history create a fun mentor program assist with different situation with the teenagers problem going on with them in life the student play high school sports take them on their college tour visits by me that in mentor program also going to watch ever game they play in until they graduate if they choose leave school early for the draft going to call talking about being a professional athlete however explain different life changing things that going to change your lifestyle with money endorsement deals with shoes cars insurance home insurance buying cars living on their own athletes will get receive invite television show advertisement clothes shoes headphones food ideas attend Espy award show and other event after finishing the season. Also super star athlete advertisement cell phone jeans have a small role in television series show and movies going to schedule camping hiking travel to different states rock climbing zip lining events going to take mostly doing the summer every summer while high school students out of school going to enjoy new hobbies never did before at all program going to help single mothers that don't have both parents in the house since giving birth to their daughter or son have some of my friends mentor high school kids a about life after high school kids a about life high school enjoy college life in their early 20's just give simple example learning things on their own time since didn't have no father figure at all since being a baby in the 90's just know a couple thing about my dad have a half-brother on my dad side of the family never meet before want to meet him in person one day. Really don't know anything about dad family at all just know a few thing about my father will not forgive him at all what he did to me being a baby my father was on drugs really bad at the time my grandmother find out smoking crack at the drug house want to make a different with mentor program single mother that don't have support from a man that choose not take care of his children at all then my mom got a divorce when I was 4 years around 1994 living without a father since being young never ask about my father until finish high school being threw a lot up and down at very young age made me to be very smart to overcome bad experience that happened with family jobs money and seen good things about bad things in life writing this book going to be the best chapter of life going to help a lot with ADHA bi-polar disorder mental. I am going to become good cook soul food and desert get another man in my life that have standards and character not stupid and idiot that not playing games and be serious with me I do believe in myself that things will change for me in the near future somehow I do manage to get my nails done and still smile as little for god life has really made me not understand why people don't give a dam about good people in this world disability has really made me a little pissed off about approving my disability check but I'm going to continue to fight them know matter what happen and come my way god love me and I love god he is my everything to me I can't forget Norma Smith and her sister how they treated me last year they gave me a little help but they very noisy and caring old women but god cares for me and my son I will to pray that one they will learn to be little more kind to people that don't have a lot of money personal things. Because I'm not in this world but of this world living life the best way I know how the preacher said to better not bitter with the trail of life he is so right about that my don't care how I am making weather not I have lights or gas or water and water but they say they love me but the as just something they are just saying because they don't know to love anybody even me I 'm a niece to my Aunt Margaret Davis, Clarence Smith, and Sandra Horne, Sharon Ransom Leon Burgess and other on my mother side of the family etc my son said that I'm pissed with them not really just real talk about my fake ass family they have never gave my grandmother any money or do anything for and my mother try to sugar coat it but I know my family help know body with any challenges. Whatever they might be in this life alright today is October 27 , 2015 I am talking to thirty- three year old guy and I am fourth seven year old lady but he like older woman I hope that this relationship workout my life has been very complicated in the last three years know money of my own and just getting here and there is not enough I'm being punched for not being obey to god taking in a girl in my house so I can make in meets but she don't not want to pay rent she been living with me for two months now my son met on her on a dating website and she does not to follow rules in my house I wish her well in the future life he just wanted some sex from her and he got it now he don't want her anymore I am praying for my son to a women that is a virgin and not sleeping with different men she is only twenty two year Bianca Scott was staying at my house to have a roof over head but sex disrespect my house by having sex with my son while I was in the other room sleep. My son need to stop being a horny young man I love my son but he make bad choices in woman I believe in faith and god trust what is doing the right things life has a way of taking you on a roller coaster but I refused to give up on life and what is my purpose in life I continue fight for my disability to be approve I got poor circulation in the legs and hands shoulders can't lift anything heavy my blood pressure and diabetes are up I'm going to make it no matter what come my way I want to live this world is a mean place I don't know why I think that life was going to be easy got to rejuvenate myself and ask god for a do over. For 2016 my plans for what I should be doing and soon as my restaurant get off the ground I will on my way to a better life just being thinking that I should have made better choices in life base talking about men and how I date men I had Gonorrhea and Chlamydia with the men I had sleep with know I am not proud of what I did but god has forgiven me of all my sin god will keep me strong my friend Tonia is a person I will always help out once get my restaurant off the ground she is a nice person and bless her with money to live and be happy my brother Derrick Burgess has heart problem diabetes Chronic obstructive pulmonary disease and he was on cocaine he help kill my mother Margere Waller. Start my own business to have a soul food place Teontry is a Special child because of what his dad to him he will get through bi-polar disorder he is a good kid over all I love him my most important need is getting money so I can in peace to get married by time I am 50 years old he got a job Marquis hotel downtown Atlanta my bill water is $535.87 gas is $92.66 and light $82.57 god please help me and bless me financial you are my hero my Teontry T Waller today is October 16, 2015 I have decision to open up a restaurant sometime next year get a license to operate a business soul food and desserts my son got anger management problem he need physic for mental state he gets real up set and pissed off at when I ask a questions I am going to continue to pray for healing in his min so when get a family he will be ok taking of his children and wife Jeremy Joseph is his best friend they went to the same high school I am Christian woman but the men I have dealing with are loser and know good for me but believe I will meet my future husband after going on the Steve Harvey. Me and Rico is my new friend new friend is 32 on November 9, I hope that we can share a spiritual life together he call to late but I like new friend my will be died three years February 16, 2016 I am trying to stay strong my brother got a lot of health issue diabetes high blood chronic obstructive pulmonary disease congested heart failure Leon Burgess need a intervention with god because he had never lose his mom his grandparents raised him and my grandmother told him that that our mom love Rhonda more than she love derrick is my brother is a very bitter man and a shellfish person my son think that life must go the way he want it he very mean and have a lot of anger in him because of what his did to him Trey need something to take to help him mental issues to keep him come and focus he is always trying new things but the wrong things life is very hard difficult the get on my nerves he work at a temp serves for two days. And he needs a job the economic is not getting better we both need work he went to school for information technology but there are no jobs in that field right now in life finding work to support yourself he really a disability check because was on it at once appoint time my son have had a rough life this year we have a little merchandise to sale hopefully all of that will sale and make some money I blame his did for what he is going through now I keep pray us to be blesses Trey is a spoiled brat by my mother she love him so much my love for my one and only son he takes a lot time about me I need him not to put so much time in what I do or say my life is not going the way I would like it to be right now my income is zero I'm praying for money to come so I can live my life in happiness and peace I will be forty seven in three months I am so bless to see it my son love me very much Trey does not know any of his dad family he has two aunts and a uncle another grandmother she is a drunk and not a very good mother or grandmother some other cousin on that side of the family. Trey got a loving god dad he is married now this is his second wife I try to give him good advice on life I let a girl stay with me and she does not want to pay me and I let her stay here with me she is trying to move and not pay me for all the weeks she has live here that is not cool I pray she pay me for all the times she has been here Trey love football gamed and basketball baseball soccer games all American guy love sports I wish him a lot of success and love in life I am in the near future open me a restaurant serving soul food and hot wings fries etc today is October 23, 2015 got know today hopefully tomorrow will be better in getting some money I like to play a game on my phone because I can't afford a phone right know income but I'm praying on that to change god will turn it around I am going to be a small business own of collard greens and macaroni cheese. God will bless me with all my resources that I will need now it is god that give you power to get wealth so I am glad of god goodness mercy safety of my god my brother is 65 years but he smoke crack cocaine and hope he get clean before he died cause that dope will eat him up and shut his body parts down in the long term he become a handicap to his self Lawrence Waller my sister is a 5 years cancer survivor Alfreda conversion she is 63 years old now my other brother is on kidney failure he can't walk he is bed written I attend church at hunter hills first missionary Baptist church family has cancer in it heart trouble diabetes kidney failure today is November 2, 2015 I'm tied of bills and don't have the money to pay them but god know all my pain he see me though my heartache and pain my life had been so difficult these past years but my god will help me in my pain. So I will trust god and he will keep in perfect peace I am going to life and not died because of who god is and not what I do he is my provider peace maker healer of good things I don't what I would do if I did not have good on my side I miss my mother so much she is the one who tell me to stay strong and remember god love you know what is going on I am on the battle field for my lord I promise him that I will service him until I died rico birthday is November 9, 2015 I really care for him a lot I hope he feels the same for me he say half black and Mexican wow I was shock when he told that is a nice guy I'm going to try something new dating a younger man who I like he don't do anything for fun but watch TV and smoke and litter weed also drink a beer so I'm in a good place with him when this book is published it will be the best seller in the universes my pray is that god would move on my situation now while continue to pray and believe and trust god life has a way of bring a lot of trouble from time to time but the good news is it will better with time I can't afford a right now. But I will change that soon hopefully I will get a new phone or used phone working soon today is November 3, 2015 this is day that the lord made I will enjoy and be glad in it god is my fortress in a time of trouble my present help in my circumstances that life has brought me for a little while I'm helping my son write this book and I hope he will break bread with me when become famous peanut butter is his favorite thing to eat he also like tacos Chinese food nachos shrimp Alfredo a Italian food and drink wine and smoke a little weed he got glaucoma he can't see good I hope that will help him I believe my new love is mix man I like that my favorite show is hot bench it is three judges that listen to cases and make decision to all classes. I love the young in the restless soap opera and days of our lives my health condition is not good I am going to buy me a gun just for safety reason I need something to do make some money for myself maybe take care of a lady that need my assist at her house or babysitting I'm praying for better living just believe in my god today is November 6, 2015 I have fall in love with my new man he is a brick mason I believe that god put us together for as reason so I trust god I will be bless with the money I need to pay a tax bill this month god give me strength from day to day Psalms 37-4 say delight yourself also in the lord and he shall give you the desires of your heart I am a believer of god and his power. God will see me through this trail I'm going through now about my finance he is a good god to not focus on my problems I pray and play a game on a old cell phone my faith is the only way I will make my son is a child he has disease that deal with the mind his dad give him medication to keep him sleep and god did not let his destroy his mind he is working on his career my life will be great one day because of god and who he is thank you lord. Health issues that people really don't information on mental disorder going to create a blog on different topic tell you what new projects working on explain more details about my mentor program and my future technology business for the grand opening current just focus on my modeling career while working at a hotel until get a very big modeling campaign modeling clothes like suit shoes swim wear business casual wear after getting my modeling career going right then going to start acting in television show series and going to be in movies also want to model casual clothes as well really didn't know about herbs until grandmother and mom explain it to me herbs help the blood flow to the brain to think whatever you doing only can put herbs in whatever you are drink and buy pills going have the same outcome. Create a website for my technology company in the future didn't care about fashion as a kid always had nice clothes and shoes wear to school some student was jealous for different reasons like know a lot students and teachers got a lot of attention from girls in high school but my freshman year in high school was all right didn't focus on school work group assignment class work just focus on girls at the time was a bad boy in 9th grade for a whole year skipping class hangout with people was not a good in influence about their school would say around 10th grade got my act right until graduate from high school start paying attention in class had to retake some classes that didn't not pass in 9th grade took them classes over in 11th grade a lot of my teachers start seen my progress doing ever class work, projects, group assignments, homework bring home good grade in a long time since middle school and elementary school days had very time at junior prom had a date for the prom she got upset didn't have the right ticket to get in the prom then got upset start dancing with other people not with her all ready know she was mad for the whole night. Was taking pictures with my classmates and friends also dancing all night until it end got home stay up for a little bit then went to sleep senior year prom was more fun to me then my 11th grade prom did not have a date at all until arrive there I would say about 5 or 10 minutes peoples was asking me did I have a date say no a lot of girls told me you very nice for prom start walking got something to drink eat little of food after finish my food talking to people that I play football with they clean up real nice made my way to the dance floor it was boring for a little bit did find a date while dancing with someone that like me for a while start dancing with her all night long she start with flirting with me so we both was flirting each other then the dj playing slow music slowly put my hands around her back then she start grinding on me she start looking up at me really didn't expect that happen to me on prom night at all. So I decided to bend down little bit on her she kiss me first kiss her back for about 5 minutes that kiss was very passionate then other people was talking about it after we kissing getting ready for the senior walk with your date for all senior that attend prom I was the popular kid in high school was a nerd in classes very quiet at times then when my friends around was talking more still a little of shy always talking to girls in the hallway before going to class didn't say much to people didn't know much about until took a class with always stay after school for a projects or turning late work bring up my grade then walk to the gym play basketball for a couple hours if I didn't play basketball or in the weight room lifting weight and running doing abs workout when school was out call my friends to see where there at then go over there to play video games and chill also hangout with my girlfriend when school was out and hangout with my friends after school. Also was a little bit of a class clown in high school always joking around with classmates that know me real well did make a lot of peoples a lot in class while playing sports and after school would say around the 12th grade develop writing paper also be a better writer in school this book is going to be a great one my friend Tonia has eight children one of her kids died because she was disobeyed to her mom Tonia was raised without a mother a mother or father her grandmother raised her she is a strong person like me life has tried to throw her some curves and mountains but she has weather the storm in this life my other friend Sandra Williams has I different story she has three sons one who has Attention – deficit/hyperactivity disorder and disability and one sons lost his baby mom she died last year I don't know what happened weather she had a heart attack or something else was with her. And the last one is gay who she love very much sometime people do things because someone else does that and they following alone the pattern but my thoughts on being homosexual is it a sin in god eyes so I will not judges gay people only god my believes is for a man and women to be together in married and not playing house fornication that what people do now when they don't care about how feels about that I will say don't live that life because you will have to repent and ask forgiveness to the master god is loving forgiving god and do what you can to help someone in need of food or money be a blessings to someone who has less than you do because someone may have to help you as well everyone has trouble and storm in life don't over look anyone my aunt Sarah has 14 children's she was one of my grandmother sister her and uncle buddy I was told she love children and helping her family anyway she could the most time of trails you have is knowing that they don't last always tough time don't last but tough people do. I'm not going to let my storm get the best of me I don't know what is worst not having resources or just being in pain ok I got to see my new man on Saturday for the first time and he is really a nice man he got dreads in his head but otherwise he is real down to earth person we are getting off on the right start so that means know we will be together for a long time I hope he said that he really like me and that I'm pretty woman that deserver the very best at first I thought he was into sex thing but he surprised me he not trying to have a sexually active his mind is on getting to know me better before that happen a real lady and not a little girl playing games and telling lies being a drama queen like somebody baby daddy I'm so happy about that right now. Because the last relationship I had the man beat me up and disk located my shoulder I take a beating from that man that got of prison for trafficking drugs he did seven years in prison and suppose to do the remaining time in a half way house then he got out and move to room in house where drugs was being use everyday his was Dwight Woodard he left still on probation beforehand he got out the halfway house he was on parole but I over came the abuse and the beating he did to me then I one other boyfriend he have killed his girlfriend because she cheat on him he was crazy guy he went to prison I broke up with him because he black my eye and threat my life he was going to kill me to like he kill his other girlfriend I was scared for life not knowing this man was a killer he was in prison for two years for selling crack cocaine. He lived on Emily place he is Darrell Hill I have made some bad choices in men know more of them rico is a nice mature a working man that I really like I have date a married man to but that only last four years he Lewis Green so when people read the book they will know that I have not had a good relationship with men so I decide to let that go ask for two sent me a gentleman to me so I be love and respected and not be a woman who slept men that are no good the life of my mother she had my brother as to the age of 19 years old and she left home in Lake City South Carolina to have a better life for her son my grandma Leona Burgess raised him from a baby after my mother left him her mother she came to Atlanta GA and she work at hotel also work for Jewish white people until she decision to go to school for dietary supervisor at Atlanta Area Tech my crazy ass cousin call me on October 29, 2015 she is a stupid idiot woman asking how am I living because I have no money I don't like idiot family member Sandra Horne. But god be the glory I will make it the battle is not mind it belong to god my mother side of the family does a lot of fake people that don't communicated well with me they help you in a bad situation but I love them my mistake is thinking that they really care about me I had a thought one time to sell weed to make some money but I'm too scared I don't like jail or police or eating nasty food I like my freedom get a roommate to pay rent but black people don't like to pay they are free lower like a bomb on the street I got to figure out a way to make me some money until I get my restaurant off the ground my mother always told never to depend on anybody but god and yourself so now I'm going to do something different don't know what yet pray and ask god for guides when get me something to do sell clothes maybe be a baby sitter. Be a candy lady write me a cookbook put great recipes in the book be god servant and help how to be a minister to my niece was in the military for 11 years she was in Iraq in the war doing the war but now she in school learning another trade to manage people at her own restaurant she has a little girl my great niece I love them she is my proud and joy my neighbor has been giving me some medication so I want have stroke or heart attack because I he as he not been able to get my blood pressure meds until get to the doctor got to live to be what god want me to do in this life is to be helper and get my wealth and live abundance life job 1-6-7 job 16-16-42 the sermon had heard at church Sunday but most life concern is to be a good mother and good concern is to be a good mother and good Christian love my mother family even if they don't care about how I'm living and be a better person. November 1, 2015 church the message was preaching the right gospel from Galatins 1-5-7-9-11 god people have to save and truly in a relationship with god and show love to god children I'm working on something to help me make some money god will help me I'm expecting a miracle to come with my prayers that I have been praying it is a rain in day but this is god universe god bless me with knowledge and wisdom Rico is my new man there is a age different but he is nice guy and I like that so now we have to pray for a successful relationship and good things to happen to us. There is no other way for us to live for god and not man my son has change a little not smoking so weed and drinking alcohol tequila I'm big fan of football and basketball Deion Sanders Hines Ward Randy Moss they are my biggest fan of football and Ray Lewis I am good woman I have been hurt in the past but god has turn my ashes into beauty for me so the question is encourage myself in the lord that he will see me through my purpose in life is to live for god and love him and myself also my favorite thing I want to do is get married and get my disability check approve live a full until I get 89 years old to see my grandchildren get grown and have friendship with my mother in law writing a cook with my son that I love so much. Get my license to babysitter until I get my restaurant-going I was a girl in my earlier years I was spoiled and loved a lot but I did not push myself hard enough so now I would not have to be without money until I get my social security check started life has been really tough but unbearable January is my birthday and I plan on enjoying myself because you only live once so I'm taking on I new attitude on men my life will never be the same. School and general graduate from high school at the age of 19 enroll at Atlanta Technical College right after high school stay at that college for one semester studying computer programming then drop out of college stay out of college for about two whole years start going to the gym lifting weight play basketball one day in march of 2012 make breakfast then made my way to the gym after getting a rebound feel light head and dizzy one the basketball sit down for a couple minutes drinking water and Gatorade slowly start walking to the bathroom then I fell down on the floor got a bump on my head got up walk to the men locker room then people start asking was you all right told them feel light head and dizzy was sweating all over my body somebody from the front desk call the ambulance for me got up and use the bathroom put on my clothes couldn't not walk straight at all use the wall guide me to the door. After the Emergency medical technician arrive they check my blood pressure and heart rate for about 5 minutes walking to ambulance sit down in the back call my girlfriend at the time told her at the hospital and she told my mother for me girlfriend came visit me at the hospital for about 30 minutes then they left spoke with the doctor say have to stay overnight for a few days until be discharge nurse was getting blood checking my pee and got test on my heart the next morning really can't count how many IV they gave me while still recovery from dehydration talking to my mom while still in the hospital bed and call my girlfriend told them going to be release from the hospital that Friday night talk to my girlfriend in her car for a while until she went home came home from the hospital took a hot shower after getting out of the shower eat a whole sub sandwiches chips pickles and drink a protein shake.

Woke up the next day went to the barbershop and got some Chinese food also my girlfriend birthday was on the same day later that night got ready take my girlfriend to the movies for her birthday and she didn't eat anything at all cook her something to eat before we left out came back to my house after the movies start kissing her then playing with her hotspot rub her back slowly take her clothes then lick her neck, nipples, ears we both was playing with each other hotspots make love to her about couple hours very passion sexy a lot of four play she leave the next morning around 3 am after her birthday stop seen her in person for a while until the summer mostly talking on the phone until I broke up with her around December. Told her was not happy anymore in the relationship start crying after that happened couple days later went to a New Year's Eve party with my best friends he told me move on at that party was having fun drinking playing still texting her at the party and taking picture with friends took a while get over my ex-girlfriend had a talk with my grandmother about different things going on with me enroll at Westwood College Atlanta Midtown Campus in August of 2012 now that campus is a Atlanta campus in middle school was very talking to girls just hangout with male friends until I broke out making conversation about things about 9th grade start be more friendly and flirting to girls more than my middle school days change a lot of my ways from middle school and elementary school being a short fat chucky kid when I was younger. Grandmother feed me soul food vegetables chicken fish pancakes grits and pizza fruits eating sweet like pies cakes ice creams and gain a lot of weight had fat checks miss my grandmother cooking she teach me how to cook in middle school every since then learn different recipes from friends and my mother have expand my cooking style with own twist and flavor show my mom new things in the kitchen always go to the movies while in high school also went to the skating rink and attend the boy and girls club in middle school for the summer went to summer school in elementary school for a class that I didn't pass in school but I did pass all passes in summer school in 2000s. after my junior year of high school attend summer fall language arts in school also had to retake the high graduation test in July after summer school went to summer football workout was a very busy for me always been a busy person with school and working also running errands do a lot of volunteer work some women that use to date can't handle a busy at all cause of him work schedule most of my summer been out high school just at grandmother house for two months playing video games cleaning up my room and taking out the trash watching TV sitting on the porch talking with my cousin friends that know my family went over my friends house for a week or two did eat a lot a lot of pizza hut also Chinese food and soul food throw the football in the yard and play little of basketball in the yard. Cut grass with my friend and his step father the only thing that I did at my friend house in South Carolina was watching TV playing video games all night and morning sleep all day helping my grandmother cook breakfast and dinner teach me how to cook eggs, French toast, pancakes, bacon, hamburger, fries, grits, and biscuits had a lot of fun memory with my girlfriend before she got sick really didn't get to see my grandmother at all while in college always call her after finish with classes still have my birthday card all gradation from my grandmother talking on the phone with grandmother every week and every other day talk about different things with me and family ask about how she be feeling gave me advice about and be respectfully and open the door for women make good decision what you want to do in life and have a good career that you love to do. She told me going to be a better father then my dad until I find the right women for me settle down get married and start a family one day sophomore year of high school was really interesting with school work and dating women hang out with friends staying out late. Went to the skating rink on Saturday night and went to the movies just hangout at the mall talking to girls my mom was very over protective very much in high school really didn't pay attention at first until figure it out soon or later explain details about being very protection around my teenager years really focus on being a successful model and actor also a writer right now still going to have fun with my friends and always making new friends at different events that I be attending being the only child have different thing from a sister and brother you be spoil a lot with gifts birthday money and food as long you make a lot good friends in your life I thought going to have a brother and sister mom was pregnant with a boy she told me got abortion know the father of that baby she didn't keep the baby at all lost contact with that person she was going have a abortion with me grandmother told her keep me. Most of my friends also mom know I am difficult person some women's don't take the time understand difficult men at all get very better connecting with that guy or young teenager boy most of my ex-girlfriends will say can be very difficult person not like most guys very different in a lot of ways start knowing being difficult in relationship dating women with few in the past just want a better lifestyle also make a lot of money writing books modeling and acting have my own television show and radio station living in hood just want to make you want get out of hood for good live a upscale lifestyle in general at this point in my life starting a new chapter with a different career path going to photo shoot audition for modeling and acting gig book signing take pictures with fans also singing autograph at meet and greet events it a game call clash of clans my friends got me playing this game for a while now it very addictive game always playing it different time of the day or week. If you make better decisions when you get being a adult your life is going to change in many ways financial nicer house new car living lifestyle going to meet new people in high place that give you advice different ideas to help people I got to change my attitude about men but I have found a new man he great man I love him so I'm ready to really get know him I really hope he feels the same way about me I have something I need to do is forgive and move with my life because I have been hurt by men that don't really care about a woman I have a choice now and how I live good life for god and not let man control my destiny god want me to live a good life I love life but the last three years have been hell but god will give me all I need renew me and transform me bring me through this storm I'm in. a good place right now I wish that my life would change but I'm waiting for god guides I wish that I could change my situation life has a lot of curves the only child I have is trying my patience but I will trust God and what he is doing now in my life my son really think everything is about him so I will continue to pray because my son is getting on my nerves about this book I am helping him write. Psalms 23 say the lord is my shepherd I shall not want he make to lie down in green pastures I will fear know evil for god is with me the bi-polar disorder my son has is not a disease doctor know how to treat I recommend he continue to take herbs god will help him with this disease I will try new ideas to help me understand him as a person dollars in the bank that tramp I let her live with me and she did not pay rent at all her name is Francesia Bianca Scott she was very disrespectful my pray is that she don't like rules or know what or how to respect herself. But my son had sex with her why I don't know he just want sex from her she is a tramp I thought that found a good man to be friend with but he is not he I thought he was so now I'm going to move on with my life good luck Rico so now I will ask god to send me a good loving man to accept me for who I am because man are not real anymore so I don't care to love them anymore get me a older thoughtful man my son said that I pick the wrong kind of men so now I will focus on making money until I get a better man life will help me change my attitude forever my son is selfish when it come to money with his mother but he like to feed me food and aggregate me when I ask for money did I know I'm a blessed mother just got one son he a loving spoiled brat his grandmother did it spoiled him he act like I'm his sister instead of his mother he is mean to me. Me and my son had argument on Sunday about money issues and me helping write this biography he get tired of me asking him for money he say he now a charity case that have money to give out all the time we but are mother and son again thank god for that I love him he is a spoiled child the message on Sunday was about Jesus meet needs Luke 9-10-17 and that god's hand is one me and my promise to myself is to be a testimony for god Trey is a stubborn bull headed child he believes everything is to his way I'm going to be in the world and pray more Trey is a mental patient but he also want these his way I thought that I had found me a good guy but he want to play with me and my emotions I wish that I never knew him men don't know what they want just to have fun and don't care about the woman. What do I do men are full of do not caring how what they say or do to a good woman my son got three girls pregnant at the same time Miriah, Keisha, Taneshia they all had abortion so I don't have any grandchildren yet I don't know why he was having so much sex then he need to focus on building his career instead of having sex. Okay he told me that I ask for too much I need money for one thing or another and when I was younger my life was so much better than now I had my mother around to help and show me what to do or how to get money when I was about 6 years old until 9 years old I was sex ally abuse as a child when my mom find out she told me to doctor for the sexually abuse and help so when I grow up as a woman I would not be emotional scare for life and I will have a good life and be with a man that tall and handsome smart caring ambitious thoughtful new start for me diabetes has charged me because I can't work only doing light duty things. Change my eating habits and excise more if I can I want to be a mystery person in this book psalms 30-6 weeping may endure for a night but joy come in the morning don't weird in well doing the lord is my strength being a sales person I am going to be make it with god's help the million dollars question is what I do to make some money in 2016 sell cigarettes and candy my family don't care about me they have never love me they are selfish human being the only person that love me is my son that's why I'm helping him write this biography about us me Rhonda Waller and Teontry Waller is a smart man want to be rich by the time he is 28 years old know I wish that I could figure out a invent to do make a lot of money so I can help myself and my friend Tonia she has eight children I know people don't like to give people money now days my son has plan another life for us. In the next five years he wants to be a writer and model also a actor as well as author then probably singer and rapper manage at the hotel where he work nowhere it specialize my life has been just like a real train as ran over my body so I got to get me a job or find me job that I can do with the wisdom and know my thanksgiving was good this year another year with a great ending I must say I have been talking to someone new but he sound like a real nice guy his mother is decreased like my mother is to I am praying for a blessed and prosperity next year know step in stone blocking me to be my best I believe that men are like creatures in other words they only seek a woman they are going to take home to their mother. There has been a murder on Ezra church drive a nine month old baby died from a cracked ribs and beat up skull now the case is a homicide case the person that did the killing of infant baby is a friend of the mother of the baby he will be catches and prosecution will be reveal of the crime the baby grandmother is on the street drugs cocaine she had to other kids dfcs have taken her to girls from her one of the girls was two years and the other one is eleven months I praying for the family that they will get justice for the baby I had a case with dfcs but it was because a noisy neighbor call me child protective service on me because I left my son at home for a week until the summer camp open the next week you he person called on me because she had issues with street drugs herself and her children got taken away from her for some time until she got clean of the crack she was smoking never I would think that people would be so mean and us thoughtful of me because should mind her own business so life is going for her because she waiting on her son come home from prison of a manslaughter charge of fifteen years locked down. I hope once her son come home that life wood change for her and a little more pleasant and not being negative person because the world is what you make it and not telling a person what to do or suggest what they should do my belief is love yourself and mind your own business and affairs now I will take all the necessary steps to make my life a little bit better when my son be famous about this book I hope when someone from her family read the book they want be mad or upset I'm a nice person but I don't like crazy and noisy person talking about me because I don't do what she have done my mother would be proud of us because she did not want us struggle want us to survive in this world today because my supposed to be family is no good to us and when my son is famous and when have restaurant business going I will be laughing about crazy people. God love me know matter I don't have or do have I love god so much when I get my breakthrough I will be in the house god is so good to me a guaranteed return Luke 9-10-17 proverbs 19-17-17 john 41-17-17 god is meeting the need and he is in miracle blessing business to Trey don't know his daddy because he left in my life right now very hard to explain women that dealing with bi-polar disorder also ADHA disorder as well when I find that special women in my life have one on one conversation about it she what they have to say about it I been dealing with this disorder every since I was young kid they only way control this mental health illness is listening to music eating blueberry take herbs also smoking weed help too if being having anxiety problems and depressed I have a anger management problem with mental illness when I be singing through my pain and struggle happened in my life. When I was in college studying Information Technology at Westwood College at the midtown campus now they move downtown Atlanta seen my grandmother died in my face it hit me really hard now in life being in South Carolina hospital I am going to be very successful college graduate being in the modeling and actor also want to write a book about my life story how living my lifestyle I love playing basketball also cooking workout with my best friend Jeremy Joseph since we was young kids like traveling a lot explore the world I have a lot friends seen me complete good things that I accomplish I seen good things in life as well bad things too can give good advice on any situation like dating, family, money, personal I am very difficult at times with my anger range on things that can trigger mental illness can act like you being a big kid all over again since you are a adult someday don't feel like talking at all cause day bi-polar disorder will be very hard with all the anger you want to forget about things you been thinking about in your mind. Well been thought a lot every since kid about learning in school it took me a while learn different from my classmates in elementary school also in high school it was a challenge I graduate from high school on time with my classmates in 2009 from Frederick Douglass high school in Atlanta Georgia I hide my disorder from a lot of people soon or later they will know but I act like regular kid growing up in school and in the neighborhood my future wife will know all about this illness how accept this about me sometimes when I be singing sometimes feeling much better with a lot pain been release all these years I am very intelligent person who want to be successful in the modeling industry and actor I will start my own charity for mental illness kids as well adults that need help with school sports education community service donate to my old high school and middle school also elementary school. Being in college was a big test for a learning experience with college work as doing a lot of community service with Westwood College I had pretty cool experience as well full time student college is mostly time management a lot research papers and projects I did a couple groups projects my grandmother told me go back to college drop out of college for a while until a pretty good conversation loving grandmother she passed away about 3 from now I miss my grandmother a lot she teach me about to be a man that I am today since I didn't have a father in my life at all mostly had teach myself how to be a gentlemen to women open the door for a women giving advice to all my female friends in my life right now I love all my friends as well females too my dating life with women didn't start until would say high school about the 9th grade or 10th grade I had very bad experience with women in high school but when I got in my 20's better than my past relationships I love my mother very much she been a good mom to me since being a baby. I start using alcohol and smoking weed after graduation from high school start drinking heavy at times going to the club being at house party with my best friend enjoy the nightlife since was 19 after high school I been drunk a lot of times can't keep count anymore I am looking for that special women that make me feel happy with here every time we see each in person or talking on the phone send cute text message leave a voice mail on my phone when I am sleeping when he was little baby 10 months because he was on crack cocaine he smoking dope for about twenty plus years my pray is that my son will over adversity and his disease he got when his dad give medicine to hurt him as growing as a developing baby and human being the drugs on the streets of Atlanta is very bad and the mayor also the governor don't care about how people are killing and destroy people life heroin is another drug people is using to get high I would hope that when 2018 get here they will stop or slow the drugs game down where the dope boys can't make any money and profit off people that have been on drugs a longtime they need rehabilitation to get clean my brother is a crack addiction for some time I have lost a brother since Lawrence Waller have been smoking dope people on drugs are consume they don't want know help getting clean god help them all. The federal and local government can stop it but they are getting a profit they are making money off that so why stop it I pray that god would come and wash all away drugs from this earth now the people will be happier in living without being scared of drug dealers on the streets of Atlanta Georgia praying for god to change things in this world so it will be better for my grandchildren in the future less drugs and more love stop the violence in this life we shell over come all the negative impact on what is going on now in this world my son is a loving child he need a little intervention so he will know how to treat a women he working he is perform in being a actor and model also will be writer plus and business manager I was going to start selling dope for a living so I can have money in my pocket I have learned that life is not what you make it. It is what you do to make it better for yourself since my mother has died I really miss her I don't have anybody to talk to other than my son and to guide me help figure out how to get money but I'm a strong black woman that love myself and making money also working on me discipline myself not for man for god I will have all that god want me to have one day finding what I can do to make money legal being smart woman that I am making god proud of me and my mother looking down on me and my son faith is the only way I will make it today in this world there is a shortage of men either they are on drugs or in prison or gay with hiv so I probably will be 52 when get the man of my dreams and my son find a good woman to love and not tramps or prostitute someone who is looking for a man that got a whole lot of money I mean a gold digger my friend who I thought was a good guy he supposed me when he stop texting me for one reason or another I guess I'm too much woman for him he like little girls that play games and don't care about him I have so much to be thankful for in this life I got my health and strength and almighty father god he is guide in me the next journey in life is to get my restaurant going and be blessed with Trey book I help him write. If write about anyone I know I'm only making this book the best selling noble ever made by the Waller addition my mother will be proud of her children love them very much my funky cousin and my brother don't know that one day when this published they will be looking for a piece of the pie but they did help me when I was down and with no money but god is with me all the way family are nothing to me I only love my niece that live in Germany Rhonda Marie Hickson and Patrice Waller they are very special nieces to me my son got turned around at a early age his grandmother spoiled him but she also know how the world works every man for himself get your own money and love yourself live for god not man. Man will talk about you and put you down black America are your own worst enemy of this life today nothing personal against anybody but I don't like anybody but Tonia and Sandra other home Aleisha I wish that I could go back and do my life over again because I'm 47 years old so what now life is up one day and down tomorrow I need some way single mothers foster children teenagers business owners helping people looking for love going on date's with change their dating lifestyle if some people just work all the time don't never treat their self at all and give people a very better make over fashion wise. It's a lot of single mother out there in the world raise son's and daughter's without their dad going to be more work to providing for their kids some mothers have help with their grandmother, grandparents friends of the family and god mother also god dad with helping their children's when their son or daughter come famous being a actor model writer author professional athletes playing basketball, football, baseball out of nowhere their father pop up in the picture want to be apart in their life now because there child make money being on a television show promoting their movies television series show talking about working on new projects and not living in the hood anymore want a better lifestyle to help out there mother and grandmother that raise them a lot of dead beat father want to ask for money since you have to work very hard to be famous it take time hard work extra hours be good at your career goals that going to change your life in many ways most likely after publish this biography about my life and mother my father going to be looking for me and want to be in my life I want talking to him about putting drugs in me being a baby back in the 90's have lost trust and respect for my father. Don't even know how my dad look at all he call back when I was younger speak with my mom about something he currently living in Alabama just know his first name and last name also know his birthday never meet anyone from my dad side of the family at all just know mom side of the family and grandmother just want to help single mothers with any situation that can help them out in the long run and a lot of times give advice on life problem some of my best friends as female be choosing wrong men to date I like giving advice about men dating school relationships signs that go wrong with their boyfriend tips any situation they dealing with at that in life women always go for the bad boy type for reasons and then turn around start dating a good guy but don't understand good men that we'll women say good men are hard to find just go in right places going to Mr. right why do women stand up men for but want to text or call two hours later just you can't make plans with person it is a big turn off from women stand up men for a date or hangout somewhere to get know someone better than friends. Really don't care about my father at all since dealing with ADHA disorder and bi- polar really appreciate for my grandmother raise to be the man that I am today and also my mother have to deal with this mental illness for a very time since being a baby since my mother going thru hard time for the past 5 years start back in 2011 going to have a better life for me and mom very soon hope my mom soul food restaurants do very good at both locals in whatever side of town decide for her business in a couple years from now writing a book also working at the same time a lot thinking and time management kind of just writing a research paper for your midterm for final exam really didn't come to my attention about writing a book about my life story around September of 2015 just want to give back to all the schools that I attend for a great education is powerful and very knowledgeable anything that you want to accomplish in your life time grandmother taught me education is very important that going to very successful in your career goals having a degree teach me how to learn new things everyday of the week and be smart with make the right choices in job's and just conversation with people about any topics that we talking about. Only seen my mom crying at grandmother funeral a few years ago she always be a happy person not for a while now since she stop working in 2011 want to see my loving mother happy again her dating life is not going well anymore she be picking the wrong men making me a profit off Rhonda invention think of something to do or sell to make money out of all of my best friends the best one was Ronald he was from Savannah Georgia he was a very caring man so I will thanks to Anita Matthews for that man I had a weird thought about my life and living it is not supposed to be all bad some good take one step at a time until god give me assign what he want me to be doing having blood pressure and arthritis poor circulation in my legs and hands diabetes too know feeling in my right thumb I'm glad that my life is going not so well for me god doesn't want me to be poor or broken so I got to come up with an idea working is not on my plans for the next twenty years of my life I'm sick can't feel my fingers no matter what I do I'm going to be successful in what I do thank god for that opportunity to be a great child of god merry Christmas to myself praying for all that god has offer me will be great and wonderful for me and all the hater can step off. Learning how to promote your goals and your dreams working on my dreams and ambitious wanting to get money is a good thing what did I do to get all this bad attack at my finance but I know that through pray and believe in I'm going to make it so what is on the schedule for tomorrow selling the t-shirts and shoes this week and the hair brushes I love to cook but I break need a from cooking so much so now Tonia is going to work that is great Trey is going to work that great Trey is working on his career working at the hotel he like cooking very much my life will change for the better in the next few weeks god is able to bring me out of this attack I want to work but my hand and legs are not working for me on any day that I wake up believe and trust god is the only way I will make it I don't like seating at everyday doing not but cleaning the house and not getting paid for my services I'm going to find me something's that will help me have money in the new year 2016 setting at home is boring this is a lot of work writing a book working on this will be a great accomplish for me and Trey. Bianca will be jealous of Trey because when the book is finished and published she will try to come back to him but he want take her back my favorite inspiration is when you bounce back from adversity and failure of life I'm hoping for a good birthday soon my son he is a mean person he thinks that he can have thing has way I got to be more productive in getting money and stop getting on his nerves the bipolar disorder he got is very hard on him so he like to his frustrating out on me instead of his sperm his dad did this to him giving him medicine to keep him sleep so he could smoke crack and his dad should be punished for his crime in hurting him son but he was not in his right mind because when you are on drugs you don't think clearly so I can forgive but I want forget what happened to my son I feel I'm being punish for what happened to him I was hungry for about 6 months me and my son was at home with no money to buy food and know money to go to a food pantry for food and my family and know friends to assist us and put food in the refrigerator and I know lights in my house for about 6 months and know gas to cook for me and my son. My friend Tonia let me cook at her house and Ms. Surry did too I'm so grateful to them for helping me Ms. Norma and her sister put me out there house because they got tired of me and Trey in the rain and cold weather on last year in November and now she ask Doris to tell me call her she is not a good steward of what god want his people to help when someone is in need of food or money or just helping in any way that part of my life is over so I'm not talking to her anymore so I hope she will be ok in not seeing me ever again I prayed for better life because every for their my life I will tell them I'm good I have never been in jail or prison for any crimes so I'm going to continue on my journey because I have that taught me a lesson about how people are going to treat me I know my family is not going to help me because they don't give a monkey tail about my well being but god loves me know matter what I have done or have not done my son think that I'm supposed to write this book or assist in writing this biography I'm hungry all the time and cant think very well I believe that does something to your brain it hurt you in so ways but I will make it I'm planning on selling this house we live in because too much responsible and plus rodents get in the house because of my stupid neighbor putting old wood and paint buck in the back yard of the house he is working on now plus we have a wooded area in the neighborhood. He a stupid person know money to pay the bills and take care of remodeling the house the social security people want give me money yet because of they think of can work but they will get a crack head a check because that's a disease because of they are addiction hopefully 2017 will be the year I get my disability approved my life has been like I have been hurt by the system is broken but god is able to do above all you can ask of him I am planning on going to Las Vegas in the future just for a vacation some me time this world is not my home I'm a pilgrims traveling this world for a little while thank god for that know body nose the trouble I see but Jesus live though it James fortune say in his song that you can make it trust god continue to pray and believe that god see you and he will trouble the water in your life just being in good sound mind and body is all worth fighting for to see Jesus one day yes I'm please in with god to help me in my storm of life and be a good servant for him that he will get all the glory when he bring me out of his attack on my life Joyce Meyer say that life is beautiful because god is our strength when you don't know who to turn to or know what to do just know god is going to see you though your trouble of life psalms 46 say my lord is my strength in time of trouble. Do you know that a cousin of mine said to me that I wanted her to take care of me she got wrong miss conception of what should be done and it is not about taking care of me she is an idiot stupid person that needs a reality check on her crazy mind that she got? She will never ever see me again but when she do I want my name to taste like dodo in her mouth family is the worst people in the world to think good of ex special I will overcome negative thought Sandra Horne will never know what or why she is so stupid because she is a black women with no heart any my stupid selfish brother Derrick Burgess he is cold heat less person never have any love for my mother or his family he has always been a died beat dad with no meaning to life a idiot person he will never know the meaning of love because his dad said when he was born he was a basted child and he was not his son he a drunk a cocaine addict and always will be who he is nothing know good to children or grandchildren in this world but I have love for him god bless his evil ways and his sins my dad family is a little different but they don't believe in giving to family they everything for their self but good people in there on little ways love them to god bless them as they live to honor god and help the needy people in this world and not the greedy now is the time to get myself together for the future. It is so great that Jimmy Carter is cancer free that was a miracle from god bless him and his family going to bigger and better things in this life will be worth the heart ache and pain in my storm of life my test of trails I wish my son wasn't so mean to me he have a attitude problem so I will pray he change his ways of thinking and doing business in this life don't you just love crazy and picky people they are not buying anything so they are asking for stuff they know is too high in the grocery store or in a department store but they people that is spoiled I'm going to change one thing something is weird in this world but not extraordinary to be something you think should be for a person who is in the church and always praying all the time not exempt from having trouble in your life or world but god is always on your side glad that I know god for myself good thing always come to those who wait I'm waiting for a miracle for the healing of my foot and diabetes also fibrosis my hands then legs camping up all the time what is good for the geese is good for the crazy people that don't have a heart NCIS in New Orleans is my favorite television show are Chicago fire, Chicago pd NCIS Los Angles with my guy LL cool J people are so set doing what they want now days know what matter is living a good life and living for god and not letting the things of this world control you or destiny. I got a lot to live for and I'm blessed in the field also in the city the real things is not letting what happened in your past and be the end of your life this journey I'm on is for Rhonda and not my family then family don't control you also can handle whatever come my way what don't kill you make you stronger love myself and love to Teontry need to learn how to patience with his mother and people I have learned that life is not fair you have to go and get what you want out of life you can't wait on the government for your money you have to take everything you need and desire because white people have been stealing from us from the beginning of time nothing too people but my Africa American they are money hungry ex special preacher and people god word god I've to the needy and not the greedy help people stop talking about it and do it not be a hypocrite because I know that god is looking at your heart and not how much you make or get or rob from people in the world in your everyday living so I don't believe that people really want to help a single mother or dad on holidays they just doing it for publication of doing things for people who doing have any and when you attend a church it should not be about how much you give but give your all and your 10 percent and if you don't have a income then you pray for god to bless you so you can pay your tithe and offering and not let the preacher think it is all about them and telling people what they should be herein practice what think preach. Steve Harvey is a nice person he always helping couples and ladies also young men in becoming a man he should get a award for his heart and his kindness courageousness watch his talk show every day he is making his mother proud even though she is in heaven I hope Steve does not be mad that I wrote something in my son book he is a big fan of Steve people should one another and not be killing each other it is about Jesus and not you your problems and circumstances trails and storm of life you can live though it I love to see people helping each other and not finding ways to take what someone that have worked for what they have worked hard for what they worked so hard for Dr. King if he was living he would be trying so hard to stop the violence and keep the peace he did not believe in violence and young men out in the street of Atlanta robbery home invasion rape and child molester smoking weed making babies that they can't take care of their self put a man or women in the white house to do the job of the American people deserve and not a person who promise you something and not do what they are supposed to be doing for the American people of the United States of American having a hard life for the last three years ever since my mom died it seem like I can't get the money I need and someone is trying hard to keep me down and out. But the devil is a lie keeps press on in Jesus name I'm going to make it and get that entire god has for me always know that all my help come from the lord you can live and trust god in all situation people in this world got know love for you and don't believe in giving or helping others I believe in myself for what will be doing in the next twenty that don't want to get married at all just want to be friends in the friendships one of the guys she dating in the past out of jail don't want to help my mom to have a better relationships and friends with that person ever since I was younger

Tragedy and Triumph

around the age of 10 she never stay in the house at all but now she be in the house watching TV and sleeping a lot taking one day at a time doing the best I can for myself and mom until my career goes from the ground up making very important business move with photographers directors publisher also going to business meeting that will change my career for the rest of my life that is a big contract going have to training for a movie role also go to the gym stay in shape for runway shows photo shoot and auditions always give a 100 percent in every audition that I attend for model gigs and movies television series show my mom also myself been in abusive relationship only been in two before and she only has one a few years ago it been a longtime since my mom been married over ten years for some reason my mom have thing for men been in jail or prison for whatever crime they did in their past. Since good relationship with my mom with her boyfriend's had some bad experience with men that different go while with her at all in the past but future boyfriend going to be better for her dating seen some of her ex boyfriend was cool with me it was a few that never get along with at all got into fights and arrangements for different reasons about things going on with my mom or about me they didn't like period she had a pretty good relationship with one guy when I was in middle school they lost communication for different reasons in the relationship the only father figure have grown in life is my god dad since the 90's being a young boy never have a relationship with my father and some mothers call them sperm donor just plain dead beat dad my father was in the navy for a couple of years before he meet my mother and he was on drugs real bad with crack cocaine until grandmother found out about it then my got a divorce then she became a single mother of one boy dealing without a father can be hard not easy to deal with it at all just have to learn on your own time understand difficult things as a man also being a teenager on your good day's or bad on life and taking more responsibility on your part that life can take you different places you want to go. It been many times went thru hard also scary time the only time that happened in high school on a Saturday night heading to the movies on the phone with my best friends decided to walk on the train track also got to the train station was on the phone and mp3 player at the time then look up somebody out of nowhere came in front of us myself also my best friend got robbed on the train track they took my wallet cell phone mp3 player and took both of my mp3 player also my friend cell phone then his money too if I took one or two more step toward the robbery he was going to shoot me just had a adrenaline rush doing the whole time could be dead right now but I am not thank you god that I am alive on today very blessed being threw a hard time with that process it took a very long time forgot about that situation every now then have anxiety attack in my sleep be shaking sometimes when I am sleeping really don't know only cause of this disease that I have with ADHA disorder and mental illness unless difficult for me telling people about this illness to my friends that know me very well being keeping this illness a secret for a long time since being a young teenager people will understand my situation some won't believe it and some will take me as I am. I am still a normal person in life but very different then other people in a lot of for difficult task people couldn't handle at all one time want to know how would women mostly think about mental illness men that difficult talk about to them in a relationship that going very well since day one when we first started talking to each other more than the friendship level probably a lot of men in this world today have a hard time explaining with their girlfriend or friend's four months I will be praying and working hard to get money to help me have confidence in what I should be doing to make me happy and god will do it when I was thirty six I was in abusive relationship with a man that I thought I knew he got on crack cocaine and hurt me bad and when I was six until I was nine or ten years old I was molested but I'm over that I ask god to help me and he did I got ashes for beauty go help me working on my dreams and myself is a journey for me but I love it I love myself and working on my dreams and ambitious I have a great plan rather I'm not taking the glory it is all god doing not me I have tried other things but had to show me he is in control of everything and my destiny if I had to do something out of the normal like selling some weed until I get my breakthrough or business stared I don't like being broke or without money. Just 25 thousand dollars is all I need to handle my business 2016 will be my year of prosperity so I'm working real hard on myself and thoughts living in this life can make you or break you I plan on selling my house I live in and move forward in my dreams and goals my son is planning a big thing like doing three different jobs like on the future he is going to be a writer and model actor which one who makes the most money for him and me getting a husband Christopher Jackson is my new friend I hope it work with me and him I can't believe people let their your babies watch empire that is a show for someone who is twenty one or older people got to get back and not be friend with their kids and be good parents these young people with children are brain died and stop worrying about the man instead of the children. Children are more important than the man so young mother get it together I wish I had the space to adopt some kids and just give them a lot of love and teach them about life I will get through this test I'm in now 1300 hundred dollars is all I need I am praying for something good to happen for me I will continue to pray for god goodness and mercy I really miss my mother so much life has not been the same since she died in 2 years today sermon was pray change things from acts 12-1-16 keep the faith and believe god and trust him what do you think of long distance relationship they are ok but some people would say don't do it because men are cheater and they tell lies I'm working on trying to not be so mean and get all that god has for me my dream is to be a successful business owner have too restaurants and a personal care home for adults children's with ADHA because my son has it but you can't tell because his grandmother give him herbs a lot of prayers so you can't tell he is bipolar disorder to I pray for his recovery from something his dad did to him smoking crack and not talking care of his son I think that I can do it well and still be productive my son said know I need money got to help myself with something until my breakthrough come to me it is taking me longer than I thought to get this money in my hands. I will get this money if it kill me seed principle the perfect will plan of god our lives is what god desires for each of us so that we might have divine freedom one thing we all have in common is the desire to be free we can be free sin guilt fear worry loneliness sorrow sickness suffering poverty lack and limitation of all kinds now by faith open your mind and heart to the truth and the leading of the holy spirit let me with god's help show you how you can be free life is a challenge I will get the victory and god will get the glory for all he has done or going to do my son is so sweet child Charlie Sheen should have told his former girlfriend that he had hiv instead of him getting sued for exhorted men should not be selfish and tell when who they sleep with or having sex with for protection my son slept with a girl that don't have a brain the only thing she know how to do is go to work and bath her butt and be a girl that sleep with different men and be stupid she is Francesia Bianca Scoot. Friend's family member grandmother father cousins sister and brother to really explain full details description about mental health issues that ADHA disorder also bi-polar disorders since being a baby also telling your grandparents they will understand more what pain and suffering dealing with this problem on everyday basics in life both men and women that have learned disorder going thru hard time on things that make it hard for us to learn more about just have a longer time to learn things that you want to learn but I am quick learn on anything that I do I hope that find a cure for mental health and ADHA disorder also bi-polar disorder in the future some days just want to turn off my cell phone don't feel like talking to anybody a lot of times just go to sleep all day don't pick up my until the next day that how I be feeling on some days really don't know why my mom put all the pressure on me for different things at this point in my life just tired of this struggle with financial problems that is big situation with me and also my mom growing up as a kid listen to my grandmother then my mom but she be listening to me about things can help with all her problems and situation in life reason why I listen to my grandmother more because she know more about the disability since day a lot of times you have be patience with small thing that deal with in school. Now since my grandmother died for about 3 years always argue with my mom about different things going with us really just tired of it do not like argue with her at all the way to forget about things are writing listen to music of course singing out my pain and frustration going on with my problems in a few years from now going to write a song about my life and relationships that didn't go well at all with ex-girlfriends every now then just get emotional about things happened in my life going to change my life writing this biography and modeling acting in the future probably going to singing helping with people about anything they dealing with in their life story if I told all my friends and mom though about suicide right in life stop me killing myself then my grandmother looking down on me she wouldn't let me risk losing my life future career plans that I want to pursue I think my mom don't understand me that we'll about ADHA disorder and bi-polar disorder a lot of times smoking weed be clear my mind and drinking when I go out my friends having fun don't think about anything just having a good time enjoy the moment with friends. Then ever now then get a text from my mom still out with saying I love you the only family that I have right now is my loving mother and all my friends that being know me very well miss celebrate Christmas also Thanksgiving with my grandmother still remember when the holidays come around she always ask me do you want to lick the spoon baby from the sweet potatoes pie and the dressing she show me how to cook for the first time around the holidays then start cooking for myself and teach me cooking tip in the kitchen also being a man at young age since not a father in life at all really didn't care about my father at all learn to start understanding of being a man then my grandmother give me a advice about women handling money school be a great student in school it something about writing keep me express about anything you want to talk about never was a math student growing up in school. In every math class be a average student very strong in different subjects such as English science social studies writing and reading writing is my escape from everything going on in my life right now also from my past experience with being pick on in school and bullying too some of my friend's stand up of for me until I did for myself in school never told my mom being pick on in school or bully on either until I learn to fight on my own and I am lover not a fighter but if have to fight will beat somebody up sometimes I have to explain to mom about thing until she understand things something she don't know about at all really having a hard time her complaining about money food buying toilet paper soap giving her money currently don't make enough money to give her so she can pocket money and she buy something around this summer a couple of email about the job title and job description they were scam jobs every last jobs some was offering good pay just was not legit at all first time with that experience more than likely people get scam on fake jobs mostly on the internet that is a easy way never going want to threw with experience at all anymore unless I outsmart the people that try to scam there were sending me fake check from FedEx want me cash them take a picture of the money back from there working equipment some days are very hard with myself also my mom always want have it her ways about things going on with her money problems right now her life and probably worrying me giving her money and like every day or every other day of the week they asked me to cash the whole check at check cashing place and then ask how far I am from a bank. One of the women work at the check place is a fake check it seem like they had my attention for the job but was not going for it at all I have new ideas for job's career that I loving doing like being a number one selling author then modeling acting and having a clothing line create my own business in technology also assist with my mom soul food restaurants to start it up liking buying the building pay for her business very soon probably want to create my own restaurant in different locations in Atlanta then expand different states probably overseas in the future just want to live a different path with job's when I have my children's in the future be born giving life for the first time so don't experience living in the hood like I did growing up as a young boy just want my kids experience better life in many ways that can be very successful in their career path when they tell me after completing high school and college they will be prepared for choosing there on decisions in life start making there on money and picking a good job living on their own don't mind helping with my kids with any problems or questions they might have one day for me and my future wife. Around Christmas time always be very different without my grandmother to spend it with be feeling kind of sad but I have my mom spend Christmas and my friend's one of my best friend live in Shreveport Louisiana her name is Shonteria Washington been friends with her since I was in college around 2012 she was like 17 or 18 at the time say I was 22 or 23 she want to be a relationship with me told her do not any long distance relationship anymore since the 12th grade start giving her advice about men dating tips life experience that very difficult to handle on her own time been friends with her about almost 4 years now we never seen each other in person before at all because I don't have enough money to buy a plane ticket or bus right now she always ask me when I coming to Louisiana one day trying to get her go back to school finishing college and she still young living her life for her future career plans that she want achieve in life also she had a crush on me for a while until she started dating in her state again she a very loving caring person also a good friends and down to earth out spoken intelligent very smart and hard work anything that she like doing that have a passion for want to accomplish in life she give me advice about my dating or if I have a girlfriend at that time probably going to start back dating in the future just not right currently just focus on my career that going to get my name out there. Ready to get my career going for me to be the best at my craft in writing modeling acting future business owners having my own restaurant's business and jewelry line probably start a sunglass line that is very affordable prices with my clothes sunglasses jewelry technology products when I create all this line in the store want to be very successful business man with all my products in the future still mange being a very good model author writer actor when that time come will be prepared mental and physical also career focus always been a very career driven person since starting college at the age of 19 then I had a setback what I want to do in life start having a big passion for writing as a freshman in college every research paper that I write was always 100 percent effort from the first word to the last word and beginning to the last page of that assignments or projects would say a lot of times people don't realize of the good moments from the bad experience just a knowledge living for the moment a lot of times start getting depression will start feeling down about yourself or life choices it was many times start going to Morehouse college playing basketball in there gym just playing basketball on different days didn't have classes or had to work then starting showing my state id to get in the gym most of the time start lifting weight for about two hours then play full court pickup basketball games playing basketball with Clark Atlanta students also Morehouse the gym also be pack on Friday afternoon sometime at night. Every now then ask some of the students to let in the gym just want to play enjoy a good games of basketball when I didn't have no school work or homework most of games I play in made all the points and give out the assist and some rebounds most of people guard me playing tight defense and coming of screen for a open shot with nobody playing defense on me some games didn't score just play defense got other people open shot just rebound gave out a lot of assist play a lot of basketball at the YMCA gym on the Southside town in Atlanta before every game that I play do about five minutes stretching then start listening to music shooting shoot until I get warm up pretty good one of person that I play with is a women she play semi pro basketball overseas in different countries so I challenge myself start guard a semi pro player that play at the same gym went to for about whole year improve my basketball skills since high school days at Frederick Douglass high in Atlanta Georgia it took a lot of hard work extra time with dribbling crossover moves shots of the dribble and fade way shot with a hand in my face growing up as a kid barely know about to dribble mostly was a good shooter then want to be a around good person playing basketball on the court so I a lot people that be playing basketball against now have a difficult type guard me always be that person to see open first if nobody not going to create my shot the female semi pro always teaching me new defense technique since I wasn't not a good defense coming off screen and roll one day she seen me playing one day at the gym told me was a good shooter anywhere on the court her name is Azzie we start guard against each other to improve both our offense of game overall. Then start picking women's on my team of course always pick Azzie on my team and other people that I play with all the time don't really say that much playing basketball at all I am quite one playing basketball let my game do the talking on the court the only when I talk play basketball with my best friend from my childhood is Jeremy Joseph we always talking about different things going with my life and his life as well too every time that I make the game winning shot against my best friend or other people's that I play with that shot is for my grandmother R.I.P Margere Waller always coming up with new ideas for myself and mom get out of the hood for good living a better lifestyle to make a name for myself in writing books modeling acting also be very successful business owner in the future basketball is a great way to forget about my past that happened in my life since being a baby a living with mental illness all my life and balance with my ADHA disorder as well bipolar disorder a lot people won't believe me if I told them at point when I am ready to talk about it cause I act like a very normal man. Who is crazy and didn't teach her anything that will her in life why is it your family don't like to help you out when you are struggling in your financial my brother and my cousin Sandra Horne my aunt Margaret and Clarence don't love me they have never did anything for my mother and grandmother my brother is sowing bad seed because he don't like to give anybody know money or take care of his daughters my mother take care of them and their birth mother take care of them until she passed away I hope that one day that he will get it together before he died he don't know how to love anybody like his children or family period we have never been close my other brother is noisy and don't think about know body but his self he is sick now the doctor mess him up I pray for him and his soul because he don't know anything about caring about family or a half sister sorry need to find something to help in mind and make peace with god Trey is a stubborn man my birthday is January 6, 2016 Elaine is my brother mom she has sleep with different guy when she was with my dad he was not a good father but he paid for his sins and miss. And bad thing he did when he was living everybody make mistakes and she was a liar to my brother told him that our dad did not take care of him he got a check every month like I did Almotus is sick now I remember when he was up walking around now he can't wash his butt now you reap what you so he will always think that he is all that now life is different for him because of how he treat his family and people in this world life is going to be good for me but most want ever see me again in this life sorry that he is sick and can't walk anymore I love him my supposed to be family is died to me the only family I got is Teontry that's my family my world and hopefully one day I will be married again Christmas is here now and I don't have any money but a lot of problems so I will be thankful for Jesus birth and keep praying for a miracle for god and blessings to come and I miss my mother so much I wish that she was here with me so we can talk and go back down memories lanes about old Christmas it was good then now Christmas don't feel any more I'm just living for the moment life really showed me how much people care about you they don't got to get it the best way you know how but don't hurt or rob anybody because that would not be right way life make you bitter and sometime you don't understand what god is doing my front yard need raking now and my bills that is past due is heavy on my heart but I know god has my back and he will fix it for me soon faith is the only way I will make it in this life. I'm spending Christmas this year with the Slogan family this year with the slogan family but on Christmas I use to be very depressed and not wanting to put on any clothes just in the bed or just watch TV all day I'm praying for a better new year in 2016 I love my mom very much she will always be in my heart Anita Matthews sleep so much until she is sleeping like a bear the in a deep sleep so now it is going to be 2016 I'm going to make it in the new year my life has been in a turmoil since my mother died 2 years ago I think that the enemy want me to be without any money or have a prophecy but god is able to do above all you can ask of him I will get through this with god help Teontry said that he got my back I know longer give a dam about my family and I don't have one because of how they treat me only my son and god I have a new attitude on life for my future god loves me Rhonda will make it with god help for it is worth life is good change my way of thinking. And nigger are no good they only want the cookie from you and to have a place to lay there head and eat sleep poop so you can clean up after them men are punks sometimes I wonder about my son what really happened to him money is the rule all things in life material things should not be your whole life just enjoy them while you are living Teontry got a job I'm so happy for him he will be working again thank god for that now it is time for me to get me a job life is going good now through it all I'm going to make it somehow my family got a rule awakening my retarded cousin think that I need her to take of me I don't she is a stupid idiot fool her brain is dead so I don't need her to do nothing for me idiot crazy fool. I hope that no one have to wash her butt or take her to the toilet because she is stupid or get sick again with her dumb idiot husband I thought family love family but I cannot she a pig I don't wish her any bad thing she and stupid I hope if she read it that she will know how I feel about her I don't like her she can kiss my grits in all areas of my life my brother will need me one day but I want be there to help him I hope he suffer for all the low down dirty stuff he has done to his mother and grandmother children mom he is a selfish sob I can't stand him he make me sick to my stomach sweet sixteen is coming a new year praise church was wonderful pastor Christopher A. Wimberley is a man of god that brings the word to the members in church he is follow god's word and the calling to preach god word to thousands of people he follow the spirit and not a min the miracle will happen if you just believe my belief is to trust god and not man he see you though any trail and storm god bless me and my son faith is the only way you see god purpose for your life may god continue to answer my pray and deliver me from the sale of this life may god continue to answer my pray and deliver me from the sale of this life my family has never really gave me money but my cousin make me sick to my stomach my source of getting money is me going through something but the reward is god will show me how to get money. What is going to be a good and not evil though working on myself and going through life struggles and trails but I will make all the necessary changes to be productive just knowing life will have you up and down want to give up on life throw in the towel but god said he will be with you until the end of the earth when you are born in this world when you leave this world you will leave with nothing having to go and work for everything in this world and get sick with no money to live on and know family for support but god is there to help you make it financially in this world my son is the only one help that I got and god living without resources is so hard sometimes I feel like know body real care about me and my circumstances and situation I want people to know that I'm strong not mad at the world but thrilled to know that trouble don't last always Romans 8:28 help me and what life god will do for me forever

I have really thought about doing something out of the ordinary like selling dope to get me money but I refuse to let life turn me into a bad person and do wrong god will not approve of that there is one ratchet person I know she have slept with everybody on her job she got luck and got a man to love her in spotted of her foolish way and sinful ways nothing but the blood of Jesus that make me white as snow there are things I need to be doing for a god and that is living life to the fullest live like it is my last day's on earth I will get all god has for me always remember that god will never leave nor for sake he will be with me until the end of this world. The enemy is dead my life went downhill after I got sick and did not save any money I did not think that I would get sick at a early age so I did not save a cent and I have been suffering a lot from not having any funds to live on when my mom died I was devastate and heartbroken for a longtime and really wish she was here to give me some advice I love my mother life is going not so well because I need stability in my life and being able to do something for myself beside ask for money from my son and being a beggar my family think that they would be taking care of me instead of helping family out is stupid and crazy idiot and they don't want to help my brothers has never take care of his daughters are help his mother pay bills he think he should live for free and be a free lower but I trust god to sustain me and bring me through this in my life I know you have to be determine and don't give up hope and believe in god and know that you will get everything you need and desire in this life with god help see you are strong in the lord faith is the only way you will get all he has for the love you know matter what you have done in your life everything will work for your good your trails come to make you stronger god will make a way just trust and believe in his word take him at his word he is god he don't need help from us just patience and believe don't give up on god and your situation. And what the world say so whatever it look remember god will bring you out amazing grace how sweet the sound my son is real crazy and he act a fool when he is hungry and thirsty once he gets food in his stomach he is alright and eating blueberry help him also with bipolar disorder I'm the only one that understand him and his grandmother but she is died now my brother does not care about me just his self and my cousin Sandra is a retarded idiot woman I hope that she don't ever need help from a family member on washing herself or just needing help in general and don't be a selfish person I hope that my life will change for the better and get me change for the better and get me something that I can get help me to nature my life and soul I always wanted to be a police officer but now I want be able to catch the bad guys and help clean up the street of Atlanta that was my dream job so now it is time for me to get off my butt now and be productive person every day is a challenge for me because I can't do much work other than talking on a phone or sitting with a elderly person my son told me that he is going to show me how to make good money and become comfortable living Teontry Waller want to understand why his dad try to mess him up wild he was doing crack cocaine and do want he wanted to do he don't think or care about him he has a serious drug problem but the good news is he is getting better with time and prays and herbs there mental health program for sick people that have bipolar disorder and ADHA disorder but the doctor like to give them med instead of herb work better what's on the schedule for tomorrow writing a book was challenging but very good for me and my son I believe he deserve the very best in this and I do to so I'm going for everything god has for us to get and more pray is the key to all of your trails and storm in this life for the past last three years have really been hard to handle but I'm praying my through it so I want to give up on myself and what I have to give to make it I was thinking about going to become a stripper or do a escort services so I can make some money and not have to brother my son for money all the time. In this mean world people and family don't care for you they just pertain and fake it say that they can't help you but they those little words I love you but they really don't they are liar to your face and believe me they go to church and believe me they go to church and service god but they don't know what god words help god child if you do it me you have did it to the lest of the that means don't be a hypocrite I a lot of people go to church but they don't practice what they preach American people rather talk or disguise your business with other people and put your business in the street I'm so glad that god does not work that way when he gives you help and bless you with what you have been praying for. I know that my mother is looking down on me and god love me very much I love god and trust him that he will turn everything around for me this is the year to shift forward and being productive and know that I'm not living my life in vain god tells me what to do and what you should do in your life having to I had another good conversation with my mom about my grades coming home bad grades I was walking the hall a lot in 9th grades hangout with the wrong people cause since everyone knew me very well at Fredrick Douglass high school also get of trouble for reason they let go cause always came clean what I did really start doing class work in the 10th grade and project I had a meeting someone about putting me regular education class in high school I was acting like normal students until some teachers find out learning illness cause my 12th grade math teachers say he very student passing with a high b average I had escape with fitness about in 9th grade start playing basketball in physical education class after school always go to weight training start getting healthy lifestyles as well being fit was not a short chunky kid anymore there is a new side of Teontry didn't realize had a six packs in the 11th grade music basketball, football, fitness, baseball, track, and field can clean anyone mind that has been through rough childhood in life I could be professional basketball, football player by now didn't start playing sports until 11th grade I should play in the 9th grade couldn't grade point average was good enough to play yet. Seen my childhood bully around my early 20's so he say damn you big ass he'll he really don't want to try a 6'5 200lbs nigga he still looks the same to me cause if he did try me would beat his ass down the whole street until someone pulled me off him give him two black eyes for picking on me as a kid then break his dammm neck!!!!!! I am very funny cool laid back kind of person as well willing try new things in life I just have hustle ambitious personality honest always very nice to people my friends, family I like helping people that need advice about anything big situation or little things going with them always keep my friends laughing and smile just a funny person getting from my mother I just want get out of hood for good to be better my career in writing actor modeling also have own my television show wish grandmother seen me graduate from college passed away about 3 years I have a passion for technology with company, laptop, videogames, cell phones, tablets any electronic devices achieve goals will not stop anyone to get that dream achieve also complete task for that person people who don't have a idea goals in their life always will be stuck with that situation for their life make sure you have a goals set in your life to be great person I start dating about in 9th grade then prepare myself with women about their feeling talking about sex hangout with them only date three girls at my high school cause it was a lot of drama who dating or you trying to someone else boyfriend or girlfriend girls fighting over there boyfriend some in a gang have a beef with someone that don't like them my high school was known for fighting or gangs fight school was on the news a couple times my high school is not the same anymore at all things have change after graduate from high school in the class of 2009 you will see fights in the cafeteria outside gym in the hallways some in the bathroom and classroom I will always love my high school I had a girlfriend at different school I play football, track and field in my senior year of high school I had two abuse relationship with them one always slap in my face broke up with her crazy ass then she came to my house want to forgive her but told her he'll naw dump on her on valentine days she was very aggressive behavior in the hallway she slap my face really hard so was tired of it told her we are friends then she trying get her mother to save her that didn't work either at all she was being too aggressive and anger problem then always beat on me. Unless I think she went gay or lesbians really didn't care about that relationship then another abuse relationship was good at one point then she start acting different always hitting me in my chest slapping start argument about simple thing little problem going on the relationship that lasts for a while until we can be friends she just want to hang out after school cool with it a lot of times have been real trying to be a good mother to him when have a disease explain why he got bipolar disorder mirrio daddy was doing crack cocaine and abuse him as a baby he was not a responsible parent grandmother and mother gave mirrio a lot of love he really needs some herbs and ask god for guides and strength to raise him right and in the church I hope and pray for mirrio to be successful in life come down with his disease I want him to travel the world once he get his career off the ground being a technology and model writer be the best you can be mirrio I love him very much mirrio want fame and wealth have been in jail because I had broken the law to provide for mirrio but he still loves his mom his died beat dad was in prison for arm robbery about 5 years his most important ambitious in life is to be a better man than his dad in the future have kids be happy married man with a special women in my life I want to raise my kids with their mom and dad go to their basketball games or football games any events at their school. In a few years will settle down from now with a special women I just want to better then my father in life with goals living better lifestyle I wish had a better family member that who communication with me and mother a lot more I have family on my dad side of the family and granddad never meet them before at all they only family have right is my mother and friends too my mom say act like granddad as well my father see the different things she talking about I have family in South Carolina and Florida I want to travel the world see different states and country learn about ethics background in Paris, Brazil , Italy, Russia oversea people have better place to relax for vacation to clear their mind ready to start my career in writing modeling, actor, technology I major in information technology at Westwood college at midtown campus in Atlanta Georgia I am very different then most men cause always be honest loyal, responsibility, respectful, nice, smart, educated, athletic, kind, funny, fun, loveable I want to buy a new house for my mom and also buy me house and jeep I want to start a charity for kids have mental health and for bipolar disorder for young adults with different illness I want to do some public speaking to talk about ADHA and bipolar tips help with kids and adults do charity basketball games for bipolar mental health illness and flag football kick ball baseball games I want to start a nonprofit organization with mental health bipolar disorder and ADHA create a contents a day hangout with me travel to out of state if they want to be a college student and take them on college tours if they are students athletes tell them what they need to about being their own with their parents be at home for four or three years of college I will visit them at their school and talk to them about anything they need advice about on I will give them my personal cell phone number call at any time for question and advice their grades have to be very good enter the contents visit there college campus don't have the money visit them at all. I have a lot planning with illness and bi-polar get more science information about different illness that can help people, , kids, adults I just like helping people in general grandmother told me help people that need help I want get my mom out the hood for good so she travels the world with her husband and grandkids in the future I wish my grandmother was still living right now but she in a better place with heaven growing up in the 90's was very cool to me as a kid it was a lot of fun memory with friends and my mom can't forget grandmother learning can give you a create mind set starting as a kid then growing up to be a adult in life I seen my grand mom teach me a lot show different aspects as a young kid and being a teenager, of course, being the only child was spoil a lot with gifts money toys birthday cards shoes video games playing video games can help with the ADHA disorder but don't too much games want be able to focus in the classroom and after school will be okay that my life is going to be great when I get the right man in my life someone who will understand me and what happened to me as a kid he wants to judge me I will not reveal who abuse me as a child because they have died now I prayed and god give me beauty for my ashes sometimes I wonder is that the reason I can't keep a man now because of that I will be okay my son doesn't know what happened to me but I will keep it a secret until I go to my grave I hope that when people read the book they will wondering who sexually abuse me as a child I'm working on things to move forward on this matter at hand my life is going to great in a few years because I will have my own restaurant and my own business for life has a lot of curves balls in it I will be okay for the last three years my life has been unbeatable god give me strength from day to day. I love myself more than ever now because all have been through in life so I will stay strong and trust god until I died I think that in another year or next year I will sell this house and move to something a little more better because of the cold weather and my stupid neighbor putting old wood and paints bucks in the back yard to help them nest my son want to move and live somewhere else in a different neighborhood he said that he went to live like the celebrity live written this book also working a hotel and model actor is his dream I hope for the best be all you can be my dream and accomplished is to be my own restaurant and help women children in this world children are a gift from god you are to love them not kill or beat them I wish I could adopted a child and give them a home a lot of love to be successful in life to be want good would have me to be life is ten percent of what you should be doing and ninety percent of what you are going to do or be so I am going to be all I able to be when I was a child my mother wanted me to be a nurse or doctor but that was a lot of study reading and staying in the books school was like trying to be a good student but I like trying to be a good student but I just did like some of the work we have to do but life has showed me that you have got to learn everything you need for life so you can be prepared for this world good thing I did learn how to be a cook and house keeper and sell make up shoes t-shirts hair brushes and expanded my thought ideas for my own business one day god give you a talent and gift to be your very best my one job I wanted to do is be a police officer to work for DeKalb county being a cop was something I want to do make a difference in the criminal justice system help them not do criminal activity all the time some of the worst murdered was done in DeKalb and Fulton county remember life never always be smooth sailing I learn a lot more in the last three years when my money because little or nothing at all being broke I lot done feel right but god will bless me with all my needs and desire of my heart. He has never fail me in this last bad years I have been living love and live life to the fullest in the next forty-years the doctors at Grady Memorial hospital are lazy and they don't know anything about your condition I have had a sexually transmitted disease from Lewis Green and Dwight Woodard they disrupt my life when I got involved with them Lewis wife slept around on him and he did the same thing he was nasty and not clean I have learned from him and would that reason I can't work because they give me a disease fooling with them and would brush my shoulders is damage real bad I can't do much he was in prison for seven years and in a halfway house he got on drugs when he moved with me that teach me a lesson about having to men at the same time good bye my life now is change what I do and think sometimes I feel a train as hit me and I am going to be in a bad situation that will keep me without money but god will restore me and my faith is strong in the lord being happy and have joy be loved by a special guy one day my dream is going to be somewhat. Men but very different from guys in the world start being mature in the 6th grade a lot of kids mature grow up in the 9th grade a lot of friends would you tell you that very down to earth very funny also smart very friendly with women some say very nice always like helping people out with about thing going with their life can be very quiet at times being like that since a kid almost have a fun side to cheer up if they feeling down on that day make my friends to have better day talking with me about anything I hope this book I am writing is going to help others people to overcome anything as long you put your mind for create your life dreams that you want to accomplish one day whenever that time come in life a lot of women that have ADHA disorder probably would need more help to control things on their own time women or men that battle with ADHA disorder all their life and bi-polar it many ways to control mental illness have to do your research and I hope they read this book have good things happen to me and bad as well still living with a different aspect in life from most guys in life wish my grandmother still living today when this book get published very soon she would be very proud of me writing a book about my life had difficulty things happened to me for good and for bad things want to make a lot of changes in life better than my father that he made in his lifetime I want children in the future don't experience life like I did since being born going to be a great father to my kid's never experienced a father in my life since being in the 1990's have to do things on my own every now then had help my grandmother and mother always friends of the family that know me pretty good of course my friends too my father try to contact my mom a few times on the house phone with had in the past then after that he stop calling the house. Want to thank my grandmother to raise me being a smart intelligence college graduate with a associate degree make smart decision in life for the long run that also she teach me how to be a unique person in many ways that you can offer women which she gave me my first name very different from most names is very unique and different as well unless I would say some women or men would understand me in my real life story probably some have a hard time believe still figure out why it is so hard for women to understand dating me really not that hard just have to take everything in about me every female's best friends that I text or call understand pretty good then all ex-girlfriends guess my previous relationship didn't want to take the time understand me very well like a book and living without a family that don't connect you at all is hard at times family that I have in South Carolina are very good people but very bad talking with myself and mom about things in their life barely see my family that stay in Lake City South Carolina that are still living in good health family should be there for you thick and thin every time battle with a bad situation to assist with your problems or just to check on you ever other day of the week wish my family have way better communication skills about themselves talking about their kids jobs personal problems health issues they dealing for advice about the situation to fix the all there problem. Before my grandmother died talking with her for a while until she got in a deep sleep at the hospital in Florence South Carolina the last word give me was you be good middle school for me was good making new friends at school went to a school dance with all middle school friends sometime I didn't have enough money to catch the bus home just to walk home after school in a afternoon school program for helping with homework class work most of the time be upstairs with my speech teachers helping with my reading spelling words going over math problems every time the teachers ask for a student to read out loud big problems with reading big words scary to read in class the only time reading out in speech class live like you don't have anybody that care about you that's hard life so I'm determine to get what god has for me I believe that life my life is supposed to living like have wealth and not be poor with a life of not having enough money to live my life because if the truth be known is every Africa American who has to work and live on pay check to pay check they living in poverty to just like me and my son so they can't get money so they can life comfortable life instead of working on a white man job or just hustle in and just barely get bye they be getting all that god has plan for your life but you have to go and get it know what people say about you if is god do it reach for the star live fear let's and get all that god has plan for your life I have had a lot though about my life and I was very grateful for what god have done for me this far my shower is broke my house needs a makeover now and don't have the money to fix anything in the house my bathroom needs it and my kitchen floor under the washing machine and Tee room needs remodeling now I have been praying for a miracle to happen not having no money and now I'm going to work for myself in something like being a business person sailing I want I don't know yet have not figured that out yet I'm a child of six kids and my dad had another child that we have never find my sister is somewhere living in Georgia but I don't know her or her mother name but I hope one day god will connect us together my dad was a rolling stone he love women and big figure women he was married three times he was not the best dad in the world he need some parenting classes on raising kids he loved children but he was a fool at times but he always remember that one day he was going to died and leave this world he had to ask god forgiveness and my mother but he cheated on my mother but he cheated on my mom with other women but she never left him she stayed with until he died. I have never really did what I wanted to do and that is be a cop now my body is getting sick I have a lot of chronic disease so can't for feel my dream job so I will always think to myself about that life maybe one of my grandchildren will be a great cop one day when I get a grand babies life has it's up and down so I'm on the up right now living for god and his destiny in this life we live god has truly show me what life can really give you so I will take it and live to the fullest of what good comes my way my mother would want me to live and be happy be blessed with all god goodness and mercy I'm child of god guides is what I need from god so he will take over my life and guide me through this storm and trails but he will get me through this and be prosperous yes I'm a little scared but I will trust god and walk with him for now and ever life never is what you want it to be but god will give you the strength to go forward I love god and how he takes a bad hopeless situation turn it into something good just one day at a times sweet Jesus my pray is to live through all of my adversity and test so I hope that I would live until I'm ninety years old god bless me in twenty sixteen and bless my son to with many blessings from him I wish could adopted some kids but I don't have the rooms are the space in my home but one day I will try to get a lest one child out of the dfcs service and raise them I will continue to get money I'm selling shoes and t-shirts hair brushes and books I'm hoping that will help get some types of funds until I really get the funds to open up my restaurant and start my business. Trey has anxiety attacks it come from his dad giving him tempo drops that is a medication you give to babies only if they have a cold or fever because his dad was smoking crack cocaine he decide to give his son med to keep him sleep so he could get high every day I would be at work and my mother would be to we really did not find out that the baby my son had been severe damage because his was only thinking of his self and getting high when started school did not catch it at first until he was getting high we was working and we did not catch him doing anything to his son I know it seem bad but we did everything we could to help him in that situation with his dad smoking dope and messing up the child because he did not deserve this I apologize for the accident to happen in our life when I was dating him I didn't see the signs of him being on drugs to harm his son now me and my mother did the best we could do for him the reality check is that my son has a disease that came from his dad did not care about his son but god will see him through this bad situation in his life strong and remember that god want put know more on you think you can bear he love you unconditional so never thin that you are a lone in a situation or something that have taken you and put you in a turmoil and depression life praying is the only way I will make it and faith I love my son very much my mother has been died for three years and I'm just really hope in and praying for god to turn everything around for me and my son so life will be different and better for us I grateful for having a house to love in but it come with problems like rodents coming in and you having to get poison to kill

Tragedy and Triumph

them my neighbor is thug life he came from somewhere I don't know he make it hard for me when you don't have money to take care of the problem right away you have to pray for answer from god and think of what you can do resolve the issue at hand what do a good person like myself do in my situation continue to pray and ask god guides thin just wait on the lord for a response. Just believe and faith goes a long way my mother always told me to relay on yourself and the power of the holy ghost he is always there to help you in any situation I have been understanding how god really works so I trust him and what he is doing in my life I got to continue to pray for me and my son so he will know that it is nothing that he has done but the power of god that he do in this world it is god power and work he is doing me and having a relationship with the heavenly father I love god and he love me unconditional my son told me that he has been taking care of me for the last three years but look at what I have done for him in the last twenty two years of his life I bear the death of pain for him when I was pregnant with him he is not understand that I need his help right now until god fix my circumstances my brother don't care for me so I want hold anything against him life is going to change will do it for me sometime I wish that I could change my situation and not be a burden to my one only son I'm trying real hard to find a way to get money for myself and let my son be stress free from my problems I believe I will live through this storm in my life nothing will take me away from the love of god in this world I know that life is going to be a struggle for a little while but I will survive this mean world with god my son is crazy he think that everything is supposed to go his way life is what you make it financially my life has been on hold I can't live without some kind of resources or money to get by on making end meets come with a price in this life today but my will change hopefully soon in the next weeks or days so I can say I made attempt to help myself in this world. My mother would tell me what I should do being doing to get things on track I love my son he don't really know how things work but he got his own way of doing things maybe he need a spiritual growth in this life and someone need to explain the way god works I get depressed sometimes but I'm trying to not think about life challenge now life is a challenge for everyone that try to live for god and doing right I would never think that I would be in a situation that leave without money and my family don't care if I'm eating or have water to bath also to stay at night or light to see in my house that my grandmother my dad mother left to live my family one day a husband. was loud in speech class feel more comfortable reading out loud that was a very big fear me to do in the classroom start reading out loud more in middle school then high school if I didn't raise my hands teacher will still call my name to a paragraph on whatever chapter we discuss in class for that day living without a cell phone for about 3 months had to used my mom phone until I get my phone back in 2014 also using my friend phone from college that was in the same class we took together living without a job for three whole months whenever had enough money went to my school just filling out jobs applications from 10am to 9pm at night then head home start getting calls back from jobs for a interview one of jobs was a sales position for AT&T stay at that job for about 4 days couldn't see myself as selling man knock on people doors about AT&T products just to make a sell before I quit that did manage to make one sale on that week after being hired full time salesman with a company after a month later hire being a customer service preventative for about 5 months it was a pretty job with great benefits being on the phone with different people about their online orders have to be very clear with details on anything topics in the call center environment and if they didn't receive their package from UPS or the post office sometimes have to check there order with a online order number before you send the package again only thing I was doing a lot walking knocking on people door do want to buy television service also internet then home phone service it was all right job for little while at times having meeting every morning before we go in the field for the rest of day had a lunch break for about 30 minutes sales job is not for everybody in the world just make for some people that have success be very detail for every products that are you sales to all your customers in different locations first time ever in my life quit a job only reason that I quit sales job wasn't for me at all first job I had at my college that I attend working in the print center associate really was a very cool for

11 months start work right after my grandmother died my job description were making copies for all students also teacher clean out the printer check for paper jam change ink cartridges replaces staples cartridges after finish with my classes work schedule was just two days at every week then if somebody didn't couldn't do there shift would fill in for them whenever that come had a lot of overtime days then sometimes I just start on my homework kill time until I clock out for work while still in class running errands for department in the school for boxes for printing papers every now then just clock in for work was really tried couldn't keep my eyes open until someone ask for print jobs had to took my lunch break at my desk early in the afternoon or few hours before leaving work. Then around thanksgiving time in 2014 my boss ask do you want more any extra I say sure what we would be doing while classes out for couple days start another job in college this was my second job being a assistant desktop & network administrator cleaning out the dust in every desktop computer change out the memory ram then check every computer hook up to the intent network administrator job was for 11 months then someone got me another job working overnight for different events when I was on the schedule at 200 Peachtree this was my three job while still in college working three part-time jobs being a fulltime college students was very time management after getting off from work just eat watch TV for a while until falling asleep then turn around get up for school it was a pretty challenge for myself to push in ways never did before in life always been very hard worker with working any that I did or just in general mostly all the jobs that I work are laid kind of occupations a lot of college students need extra money for food paying cell phone bill personal hygiene stuff or just want to have spending money hangout with their friends and come home to visit family my life has been fine for forty three years I live because I was getting money but when the decide was made that my mother was going to leave this world then the enemy to leave this world then the enemy came in like a flood kill steal and destroy my life that god had ordained for me so I have to suffer a little while but god is keeping me strong and mighty he is turn around everything that everybody set out to keep down in poverty that have forgot that

I'm a child of god so know weapon farm against me will be able to proper us in the name of Jesus I'm going through a test but my faith has brought me through hard time and storm in my life in the last four years I'm standing on the battlefield for the lord I'm still here and trusting god for what he is doing to change my situation around for me in 2016 life for me will change I know god is working it out for me thank god. I'm being patient and waiting on god for my miracle I don't put my trust in a man is a false hope and liar my belief is god always taking him at his word god will bless me financially in this year god said don't focus on the problem focus on me and what I can do when I will change and restore everything you have lost believe god and trusting him taking at his word he give life everlasting life and what could be more precious than that the ability to make something of yourself and not let the things of this world break you because there is a journey in this life you have to follow which god have plan for your life and there is nothing that you can do about it living life sometimes make you feel like there is no one who care about you and there is no just be patient wait on him he will be there when least expect it he show up and show out on your behalf because he is god and he has the power to the impossible my faith has really being tested on now but will see me through this bad time in my life I give all of adversity to the lord he will work it out praying for god to speak over my life and my situation now coming up with a way to make it until give me that relation my circumstances life have taught that you go to humble yourself and trust god wait on him to give all that you ask of him every day is a challenge but god know best for me thank you god life would be a tragedy of events if we Christian did you have god on our side god bless me and my son this year with a great ending that is coming to us I have go and get help from agency that help people with rent and utilities but I'm so glad that god don't treat you like man does he will lead and guide your footsteps and want talk about you put down he love you know matter what failure you have made or mistakes he will for your life is be prosperous and blessed in your finances and be a blessed to someone we he blesses you I'm glad that god is using me and he showing of his love for me but the whole thing is god is good all the time. Am not going to worry about anything that come my way because god got my back there have been time a though about doing something that was not of god will for me but then I had a relation on that idea and god said know you are better than that wait on me I will bless you and show you how your blessing will come to you my daughter and god block some stuff I would not get hurt or confused thank god for love grace and mercy and favor I have been hurt in bad relationship with men that don't know how to love a woman but they can ask for sex from you and come to your house and eat up your food if you have a car they will drive while you are at work working these are sorry men they don't want nothing out of life they loving on woman and milky you for what you have and like that just so they can say got man they is supposed to take of you the woman and love her not for what she got I have learned that a man should love you not beat you or ask for money I have made some bad choices in men that way I'm not rushing to get another man right now when I get a man again kids someone to love me besides god but trails come make you stronger I'm thankful for a place to live but there are too many problems and I don't have the money to keep it fix up so I'm going to sale my house and hope that someone buy it live in it also know that it want be the same problem I had whoever buy it will fix it up and live in it the way they want it to be because you can't live without some kind of resources in this life I'm not understand why my one be family really care about me and my circumstances they don't care just about their self my son said that family isn't know good to me and him but we will make it seems rough but god will see me through the valley of shadow of death that's why I don't give a monkey tail about them one day they want to be a friend with me but no way I have loved in my heart because I'm a child of god but they make you want to tell them to go where the sun don't shine cause real family would try and help you some kind of way but I have selfish family one be kin folks but they reap what you so in this life so my life is going to be successful god will do one he said in his word my mother tell me my family isn't worth a quarter or dollar god bless them in life they live my pray is that everybody have peace in their life. And if you don't know Christ Jesus lord and savior and repent of your sin and get it right with God when it is your time to died you spend your soul will go to hell eternal damnation god will give me everything that enemy stole from me praise God when God said life would not be easy but he overcame the world so that mean God has already died and raise for everything you need in this life. Life will throw you a curve ball so stand on god word and continue to pray believe trust god Deuteronomy 8-18 life is too short to let people that only care about their self I know theses to elderly women who say the love god's children don't know the meaning of the word they just want to know your business and not help you or pray for you and your situation just be two old noisy women that don't have a life other than knowing everybody business that is a sad case that mean that god will cover you and keep you from people that said they are save and feel with the holy ghost some people don't know how to love or be concern about children or doing god's they are fake people I don't like that god will bless me I know he will my son say that people should stay in their place when they are not real or know what they should do to love do something that god will have you to do for someone that in distress my grandmother always say that a nigger isn't do that means they don't mean you know good so for people that know or don't know me god bless everybody them hopefully one day they don't be in a situation that they need money or food or drink and there is no body to help them in their bad situation and they don't know god and know family to assist them and have bills and rent to pay they probably would go crazy and kill their self black people are selfish to anything that mean giving money or learning a helping hand. But god love all of his daughters and son's that have lost something in life he will restore all you have lost that's the kind of god we got god bless the child that don't have its own life is not what happened to you it is what you do to change it and when this book is published I hope that idiot family don't hate because they did not want to help us but be happy for us stupid people is in my mother family I think that they stuck on stupid and don't know what it mean to love family in any situation Matthew 7-7 Luke 6-38 Galatians 6-7 Malachi 3-10 my dream is to have my own restaurant and do well in my business and get a car see my get relive from bipolar disorder and ADHA disorder he got when his dad give him medicine to hurt him crack cocaine is a devil drug but there are people that are addict that drug his dad is a man that don't know what is supposed to live their parents' also brother sister too it very hard to work in the technology field without job experience you have to know somebody to get your foot in the door for any jobs in this world technology has change in many since I start elementary schools around the 90's now technology have everybody attention with Smartphone's laptops desktop computer high definition television headphones smart TV's. different tech companies have pretty good ideas for young children's can learn on laptops and desktop computer expand their education skills in all subjects never receive any love from my father at all no love since being born a baby at the hospital he came to see my mom but got there late really not looking for anything from my dad don't care being a crack head dad barely took care of his self I don't have any love from my sperm donor really think he wasn't ready to be a father to me at all from my opinion if I never had this mental illness would be a totally different person growing up as a kid but I am not never had a role model in my life only person was my grandmother excellent role in my life since day one on May 9, 1990 at Grady memorial hospital in Atlanta Georgia grandmother taught me right from wrong in elementary school until start learning multiple things at different times in my childhood learn more difficult things to do for myself or just ask for help one day my mom told me she seen me shaking in my sleep first time ever heard that before really don't know why sometimes I be shaking in my sleep every now than it really been a lot of pressure since my mom stop working always find ways to get the bills paid every month being in college really didn't have a choice take more responsibility on her financial crisis while my grandmother still living she always get extra money though the mail from her mom not anymore my mother really don't understand how much extra long hours to work 12 hours shifts straight just with two breaks while working. Every time when I come from running errands all she start worrying me about different things can't enjoy my dinner sometimes at all had to take very big role giving my mom money from working at the hotel always have to share with her and she be asking question without thinking about the situation clearly sometimes when we having a conversation with my mom don't want to talk at all probably going have a nervous breakdown a lot I been without any help from my family for a very time also she been putting more on me for the past four years now really don't why yet always have disagreement with my mom different discussion and very important topics she always bugging me for toothpaste and deodorant can't even have that to myself at all also asking for something every other day of the week or month always going to love my mom very much she can be very difficult at times just want to get on my nervous for no reason because I am the only family she has right now in her life passing of my grandmother for about 3 years now just really want to know does my mom appreciate that I does for her and myself could be a very good answers to all my questions for her haven't really ask the really hard tough questions to her yet just waiting on the right time to ask her. Still remember those in high school spending quality time with grandmother around the summer months one day she brought to my attention about learning about life in general being on your own different things that you couldn't do at all as child learning life experience is not fair to everyone in the world have to work hard for everything you deserve have nice luxury things in your house and apartment for yourself grandmother taught me to choice the path want to go in life with goals that set for myself trying to figure out why do people give up on their life don't want to change their self or for friends and family if you choose a bad path in life doesn't take a genius have to change for positive lifestyle if you do I love him my son is very important to me but I need that love from a Christian man who know the words of god and love not the streets have a heart for god and not man letting the streets or your what your past life you have live wanting live for god and have peace happiness in your life ask god to guides you in the path he would have you to go because your life has been in the streets for so long you need a change in your life and god knows the road you need to take and not your flesh I'm happy you want to change for the better now and let the street go Morris Rico Morgan he will learn me and thin some great things about me how loving and caring I'm. he need to pray and ask for a relevtion so he will know what god want him to do and know me I will help him because I love god and not man I'm going to get all god has for me Morris will have understand that his life is not based on what his past mistake but what god is taking him to and live for god what is your purpose in life and what you should be doing in this life god has plan for you purpose and plan for you in life you don't know but god will guides your footsteps so you will go don't right one life can good and can be very bad pray and seek your heart to find what it is that you have a gift or love to be doing to be a helping hand to life good the bad and the ugly people are sometimes in capital able of keeping their promise they don't believe in giving or helping people just talking there or some life challenge you need to help people that have been push aside and give up on life my family don't believe that life can change you or break you in some ways you have to be determine to stay strong and continue to pray for positive things to happen in this life I thought that my new friend was the one but he is pop game to me so I will just let him stay where is and continue on in Jesus name and pray that I will get me a god fairy man that will love me and know what is supposed to be doing for his queen he has found to be with these men like playing games so I will keep my distances and not talk him as much he will be just a friend and not my future husband. So keep god in the misty of all of these stupid men they like a plate of food they don't know they want to eat steak or pig feet or bologna for dinner I'm going to get myself ready for a wonderful miraculous miracle and a great blessing coming my way know body knows the trouble and trails I had to face in this last four years of my life experience not having the any to pay bills or buying food for my household or fix up the house my grandmother on my dad side of the family. It has been very hard and very difficult on me but I appreciate what god is doing to me in my storm so when he bring me through he will get all the glory and honor the pain don't feel so good but I'm going to make it through so when I get famous I will be happy and content so I'm praying that this year I get money so I want have to continue buggy my son for money and stress him out I don't want him to have a nervous breakdown or get sick and have to go in the hospital find out what my plans for the future that

I can to make money find my passion in what I love to do in this life now is the time real live for god and follow his command for this life he has for his precious daughter one thing I can say that he want let you be in a storm in your life for too long before he bring you out of it my savior is strong and mighty he want let you fall there have been some dark days in my life but god has been with me all the way I'm going on to greater highest in the lord my faith is growing stronger in my god and I shall not live not died god has a great plans for the rest of my life my pray is that I live until I get ninety years old before I died so my child the only son that I got will understand that I really appreciate what he has done for me this far until I get my breakthrough or my disability approved and stop depending on him for money he will be blessed going in coming out of his disease down but don't worry about people are jealousy of you when god give you a purpose and plan for your life. So believe in yourself you can do it there many story that people can tell and how it happened then what are you going to do about it I don't believe people in this life really know how to work or what do in a situation but to look to god for strength and help my experience in is life is everything happen for a reason and a season god bless us all sometime when you are going through trails in your life don't feel so good but remember god hand is on you so don't fear he is there with you every step of the way my family has hurt me and disappointed me I want ever talk are trust them again so I'm moving forward in my life. My life has changed in so many ways because I had to learn that people don't want to have nice things or be successful they only want what they want they don't want you to be happy or to have that love in your heart but god has power over your life and he will to love and guide in your life most of all be obedient to god and you want go wrong I know a lot people but some of them are not caring about you only to be in your business and put your issues that you are having in the street I remember one time this girl I grew up with she was always telling you want to do and try to get to do something that's not right she had about four children then once she seen that you was not going to go alone with your little mischief or do something that would get you in trouble like get pregnant or do drugs she did not care to be around you but

Tragedy and Triumph

I'm going to love her god said love your enemies and pray for those who spiteful use you so I have love for everybody that thought I was stupid or idiot but got to love yourself and don't care about what people think of you only what god think of you matter you can't live for people only for god because he has his hands on you until you died repent of sin present past and future you live a life of abundance for god so when going through a test in your life you will know what to do. Pray for good things to happen to you and for you my life is going to be better now that I have surrounding all my problems to god and I'm staying strong because my savior is with me always until the end of earth onetime I real scare of life challenge but then god spoke to me and told me don't focus on the problem focus on god there have been times when I had to eat peanut butter sandwich so I can have some food to eat my so called family did not give a money but about how I was eating or praying my bills or really surviving in Atlanta Ga they live in South Carolina I have a aunt and uncle brother cousins but they only care about their self and they say that they love me that is not love but god loves me unconditional so I don't need them to send me money or care weather I got food or my bills have been taken care of one of my idiot cousins said that she can't take care of me but I remember when my mom told me she was in the hospital she could not even wash her butt or get up to go to the bathroom my sweet loving mother was praying for everyday she was laying in the hospital sick and now she can't help her own flesh and blood but I want forget how she and my other family have treated me since my mother has been dead that why I will say go to monkey butt showcase I don't want your love I'm going to be fine me and my son will continue to make everything that god has for us to make it a finish a great life. I believe that family is a bad disease to family that don't have their own money to live off I forgive them not because of them because I have love in my heart and god told me to forget about family or want or be nigger I'm in a situation now where I need 592 dollars right away and I don't have the money to pay this bill I am praying for a miracle to happen soon to pay this bill and so I want be out doors or living in a shelter me and my son. My son think that I'm supposed to pay all the bills I really hope that god will bless me very soon mental condition that is troubling him but has faith in god and he believe he will be delivered from this bad night mare his dad did to him smoking dope and not being a father to his son instead of hurting him in the process that is not a real man that is a person that only care about his own personal needs and not think that he is hurting his flesh and blood but Teontry will make me proud and his dad will try to come out of the woods when he get famous off this book then will want to try a slick move to ask for money or lie and say he was not ready to be a dad to you or the drugs toke over his life which he don't really care for his sperm donor for a dad my mother always told me to be care of men that don't have the house or apartment to live in because they could be a dead beat man or just like living off of a independent smart woman that know where she is going in life sometime it is ok to help man if he is really looking to help his self and need a little assist from a Christian woman some men like living off your accomplishments that you have work so hard for that's not good trying to get his self in a position where he can be a better man for world and his wife and be a pillow in the community life is full of ups and down but if you would trust god in everything you do you want go wrong. I had to learn that for myself these last four years without money to support my household and ask people for money make me feel like my family is a sell out to me that why I don't keep in touch with them but god got my back and my son I have not gave on god and he still love me unconditional I have thought about going to work at a strip club that would not be the Christian thing to do so I change my way of thinking and said I would go in another direction with god by my side plus I have always wanted to own my own business doing something construction with my gifts and helping someone who have given up on life open a place to help women and children taking care of senior in their days to come letting god use me for the kingdom of god life would not be the same god will guide you through this whatever you want to do to be a helping hand making one step god will make to for you step out on faith and believe in yourself for I live for forty seven years and I'm still learning how god can move you to another level in this life and he will get the glory and honor for your success and your life man will always put you down but don't worry about people are jealousy of you when god give you a purpose and plan for your life beloved I wish above all things that though mayest prosper and be in health even as they soul prospered. 1-1-1 johns 2 god never put more on you than you can bear god can turn a bad situation into something good for you then you will say that it was no body but god working out that storm you was in your life my story is that I have not got my social security check yet it has not been approved so I got to go to sorry doctor at Grady memorial hospital that don't know how to treat me for my condition or help me they should give me some kind of medicine for my condition those doctors don't know how to treat you for certain types of health issues that you have they only know how to treat people for strokes and heart disease and gun shots stapled wounds or drug addiction I'm pressing on in Jesus name there are days when I believe that god is crying or sad because there is so much violence in this world and there is no love know body loves anymore or really care about people and their problems I mean the people in the church and some preacher they are only looking for a payday from the members of the church they bring the word to you on Sunday and then when service is over you leave go home and you still wondering how or when god will bring you through your test of trails because the preacher preach to you about running god's race and when things get rough you got to stand on the word of god and don't give up on life keep going because god loves you very much I don't have money to 2 chronicles 7-14 if my people who are called my name will humble themselves and pray seek my face turn from their wicked ways then I will hear from heaven and I will forgive their sin and will heal their land … make a noise unto the Lord all year lands serve the lord with gladness come before his presence with singing know yet that the lord he is god it is he that hath made us and not we ourselves we are his people and the sheep of his pasture enter into his gates with thanksgiving. And into his court with praise be thankful unto him and bless his name for the lord is good his mercy is everlasting and his truth endure the to all generation call unto me and I will answer thee and show the great and mighty things which thought knows not exodus 15-22 Moses brought Israel from the red sea and they went out into the wilderness of shut and they went three days in the wilderness and found no water let us not be weary in well doing for in due season we shall reap … Galatians 6-9 meditate on these things : give yourself entirely to them that your progress may be evident to all 1 Timothy 4-15 the lord is my shepherd I shall not want he make me to lie down in green pastures he stores my souls he heals in the path of righteousness for his name sake pray for one another Galatians 3-9 let not your heart be troubled john 14-1 he will sustain you psalm 55-22 he will direct your paths proverbs 3-6 surely I will be with you judges 6-16 with god all things are possible mark 10-27 let your requests be made known to god Philippians 4-6 and calls those things which be not as though they were Romans 4-17 but my god shall supply all your need according to his riches in glory by Christ Jesus Philippians 4-19 Hebrews 12-1 let me interject this thought … sometimes we feel that those who are different from us could not possibly be going in the same direction; this is a false notion people don't have to be just like you what matter is are they going in the same direction? You need people, who share directional agreement, but they don't have to be just like you; they only need to have the same directional thrust, otherwise they become weights. My grandmother that live in this house she was a secretary that loved everybody she took in some men to help herself to pay her bills in this house that I live in her husband Raymond almond had built from the ground up you can't let everyone live with you because people don't like paying rent to a landlord life has really showed me how to depend on god my real dream is to own my business and do good in my business now I have a new man and I'm praying that we get together and be happy forever he is from Savannah Georgia I have been waiting for so long for a good and respectful man to love and care for me not a thug or a dope boy or a hustle that don't have any matters my son has been helping me paying the bills in the house but he don't understand what I have been going though I don't like asking him for money or food cause he think that my finance is the reason I have to ask him for money and don't believe he giving me money he want me to get money on my own without a job income but he know that my body and is not able to work anymore I'm sorry

Tragedy and Triumph

I didn't save any money to help myself until I get my disability approved or god send me some help my faith in god is the only thing helping me not have a crazy met down my life has not being the same the last four years has been very difficult not having enough money to pay my bills and take care of myself life is not going to break me I'm strong in the lord god will see me through so I will continue to pray and try to get the money from other resources to support myself in this life I hope he is not upset with me about all I have to put on him all my problems of not having any funds to live on no money in my life. Life has not been good to me this far but I know god will restore all that the enemy has stolen from me don't have a relationship with god you not going in right path just wanted to live with the devil in your life until the day you died it going to hunt you for the rest of your life can't really tell fake people nothing in the world also trying to bring you down in life and whatever you decide to change about yourself it many ways to get out of low income poverty people just are easy to give up in life they don't put enough effort back to square one just have to say tired of the way you living if you want a nice big luxury house create different ideas for yourself when your plans come true in life keep grinding and praying for a better blessed from god somebody told me to give up in life also they say I am not doing with my life at all life that motivate create a plans also dreams for myself and mother get out living in the hood anymore when I settled down start a family want my kids living in nice big luxury house with my future wife and myself fake people they don't have a lot of friends tend to be a alcoholic in life drinking there problem away they want to be all in your business ten to be your friend but they are not your friend at all and fake people can be in church praising god and don't know to communicate with people or treat human beings in this life really still trying figure out my father neglect as a child growing up after being into this world around the 90's it is a very big numbers of the and father also neglect their children's after being in the world for the time being a person whatever path god what has in store for your life everybody mistakes at a point being young and older in life sometime have poor judgment doing bad things for a lot of different reasons it been many times though about suicide killing myself in a couple ways growing up as a young boy never have the symptoms of bi-polar disorder until I got in college start having nervous breakdown balance three jobs and being a fulltime college student in 2012 as a Information Technology major ever time start talking new women they probably thinking I am normal guy but I am not normal it very hard to battle with two different mental health illness before being one year old. Women don't care about to ask me about do you have any mental disorder before whoever want to know me it would be very surprising if women start asking me that question women couldn't believe that I have mental illness problems all my life that why I don't tell women about my mental health until they ask me explain full details about my ADHA disorder and bi-polar only people that know I have mental health first person was my grandmother she found out about first then my mother all my elementary school teachers and my elementary principal graduation from elementary until starting middle school start middle school the following year of school having a meeting with different people about my classes scheduled talking with special education teacher's then attend speech class staying after school for extra help in learning program for students with learning disorder start blending with regular education students after a long good meeting class work and homework projects start doing better in the classroom less than a month education was very interesting all levels of different grade level for me favorite schools in school were science history language arts gym class was in JROTC for about 3 years start in 10 years really don't know if my father still living at all he might still be alive maybe be dead never meet anyone from my dad side of the family at all probably will have a good talk about my father being a man and being a dad really do thankful that my grandmother found out my mental illness before it got really bad for the long run in my life but it didn't handle my ADHA disorder pretty good since I was a baby every blue moon have been thinking about if I was not mental human being growing up as young kid really think god put me in this situation going through a different phase of my life when I get older to figure out my life plans and goals. Every morning my day is getting up saying my prayer and then going into the bathroom also bathing and then going into the kitchen fix me something to eat for breakfast after that then watching television let's make a deal the price is right then hot bench sometime I watch Adams 12 but I would rather be working but my right foot and both of my legs they hurt real bad my shoulder don't let me lift anything heavy and my hands I catch cramps in them all day long know rest with my hands can't see too well so I'm just going to keep praying for a miracle to come my way because right now my son is helping me with the bills and food in the house I once was a dope girl selling a little bit of weed to make end meets I believe that if my mother was living a would be in a better situation now but I think that god will supply of my needs and desire of the heart and more because men don't like giving a good women money they just want sex and to live off of you tell you what to do with your own money you make don't like giving a good women money they just want sex and to live off of you tell you what to do with your own money you make I just wanted to be happy and live my life that god has plan for me he knows my future what he want me doing I believe that god want me to prosper in have all the richest in this world so I got to pray and ask god what he want me doing to get his wealth and all in all he is a great god I love god that my life will never be the same in this life I'm just a child of god who is just traveling this rough road thank god this is not my home to stay so I can shout out to god thank you savior bless it be until him that is able to keep you from falling all wise god that you failed he my light in dark places he give strength from day to day and you pray he will answer your call. The enemy want you to think or believe that god don't love you or he will change your situation for yourself walk you through it with you because you are his child and he is your father peace and love to my son his mother for having the courage to write a book and we are getting from a person that I have been knowing for some time my son in the bathroom and put too much it is cheap tissue and it stop up the toilet sometime I wonder is he getting better his bipolar disorder or he is getting worse I truly love him but sometimes he act like a five year old boy with his ADHA I'm waiting and wondering on god to bless me with some miracle money and blessing for my neuropathy in my foot you have to live life to the fullest because tomorrow is not promise to you so live life and don't worry about what is going to happened in your life or this world just remember that god will never leave you alone just trust in god and believe in yourself by faith you will receive god blessing and grace living life in this world can be very challenging without know funds to live off but my god will supply all you need in your living walk by faith and not by sight just believe in yourself that all things are possible with god. I remember one time that we had to ramen noodles for dinner because we had know to buy food so we had to suffer from not nothing to eat I had a abuse boyfriend for three years then we broke up after I got help from my mother was going to do something bad to him but I stop her because he was not worth going to jail or prison she was very sick the Christmas of 2006 after she after Georgia and went back home to South Carolina she went on dialysis for her kidneys had fail she is my hero I love her very much now I'm in the again without lights the money have not come on my son card so we can paid the bills I am tired of been in without money to pay bills and live my life I just living from day to day know help from my not so caring family I'm trusting god but it seems like god has forgot about us I have faith sometimes I wish I was in heaven with my mother and not down here on earth in this mean world people don't care about you are your situation got to be a better way for me to be living this life I can't believe that this same problem has come up again what is really going somebody don't want me to be happy or have peace and now I have to suffer some because my lights are off again so I have to go to my friend Tonia house so I can have some lights and be able to cook me and my son can eat our food from our house but there is one problem she have a five kids and I got bad nerves they don't like to seat down and watch TV or go play they like to eat a lot plus she is a real good friend so I'm grateful to have a friend like her. She got three girls and five boys some of them are having problems obey their mother so they are in jail but hopefully they will get out soon and get there self together and get a education get some kind of school Ged plus some college training and help their mom the system has taught me a lot to pray for and believe in my faith in god will keep me and sustain me in all of adversity and trouble I feel a failure sometime but I know this only test of my faith in god and myself I wish sometime that I have saved some money to live on so I want be having a hard time now and my mother is died March 15, 2016 my son is having to work and sell stuff out of the house to make ends meet to help me until I can get myself with my finances we have been struggling for the past these four years still praying and working hard to make don't let people in this world but my god is going to see me through this trail I'm going through I love god I truly believe and pray I will get this money to pay a tax bill and get my lights back on I am so depressed because I'm not use to being without money or not helping myself I will be so happy when god will release and let go of the money he is to bless me with and the enemy can't do anything about it I should start living on the edge and don't care about nothing people don't understand or care we you are struggling or just need a little assist in your financial situation my neighbor Doris have been helping me to only a little bit but she is having a hard time herself her daughter is on Crack Cocaine and sister brother also sister in law with three children and two people live in the basement paying rent I want to make god proud and my mother proud of me look down say she is doing good she would be very proud of me and happy say my baby is really making some money for herself. My fibrosis is giving me a very hard go around I can't even whole my urine one minute I will be so glad when I get all of my money lovely gifts that's has promise me I'm getting ready to get me a real man that will love me for me and not what I don't have and will love me unconditional he give me money for all the men that don't dog mean out and did not want me only my money or what I could do for them I have to be in my friend house and her children are really a handful and I love her she is a true friend to me I would take her for all the tea in China she is like family to me and my son who has said we are like bonnie and Clyde or Thelma or Louise she has always been there for me through my hard times I have known this person for years but when situation come up she run away and can't help me just talk trash about me I think I might going to let go she is a very controlling woman I hope she never need my help in her life because I'm going to give her a flashlight or tell her to call the salvation Army she smoke weed and do dumb stuff I hope one day she find out that cigarettes she is smoking going to give her cancer I hope it don't kill her my light bills is $263.17 and the gas is $98.46 the water is $752.48 this one bill is $562.47 but I will get through this test I'm in. life has been not so good to me but I'm not going to let life challenge stop me or break me this is my last chance to do something with my life and tell my story god will bless my hand and my house for all my needs forever love God and myself so he will be with me always forever I'm not looking for a hand out just a helping hand what will tomorrow. Helping people battle with ADHA disorder and Bi-polar also any mental disorder illness for women or men young kids teenagers adults it probably a pretty good numbers of parents that have a hard time understanding mental illness people growing up as a kid didn't tell my mom everything that I was growing threw in my life deal with it on my own without telling anyone sometimes had to ask my grandmother about different question that I didn't understand at all if I told everyone to the public any social media sites or apps that I have ADHA disorder then mild of bi-polar disorder they probably won't believe me soon then later going to be believe me I am very quiet smart quick learn tell it like it is about any questions and problems to my friends or anyone else that need help with advice how this young gentleman have two different mental disorder since being a baby really don't anyone about this once every while somebody will ask me that very rare to knowledge that question about me I have sleepless night just be watching movies playing video games listening to music writing texting watching TV singing and eating food sometimes I sleeping half of the day staying up all night being a night owl person from my mom when she was pregnant with me also talking on the phone with my friends really can't count how many times I been depressed about not having a father in my life losing my grandmother barely have enough money to pay the gas bill and light bill then the water bill too second time the light been off had this problem two years ago but this time getting warm weather in Atlanta. First time the lights was off back in 2013 it was really cold weather then glad it is getting back to hot climate change in different states second time that I have sleeping without lights two years ago don't want to sleep in a dark house anymore I been thinking about writing a book since my grandmother passed away always been a very quite humble person and not a afraid to get my opinion for any reasons that I may go have problems with in my life god is showing me different ways to get bless with and take a path with writing others things that I enjoy doing on my free time it took a very long time accept being a ADHA really don't know if women start accept for who I am just a big heart but with a two different mental all my life I am first person in the world to having ADHA disorder and Bi-polar that would be a very accomplish for me then start getting recognition about my illness and that anyone can get out of low lifestyle as long you have great ideas and plans to make a lot of money barely that you seen on a nine to five jobs also hotel job's too I hope get a lot of recognition being a good author model actor business man and probably a R&B singer or rapper one day in life sleeping in a dark house for the second time this happened to me being a young adults in life just have to make a lot changing in financial wise with a better paying job really just tired of living of living in a low income life want to live in middle class or high class lifestyle won't be worried about getting my cell phone cut off and the lights anymore. My so called friend is putting me out her house I guess because she got a ma living in sin lying up with different guys and not teaching her children how to be clean and not turning tricks with different guys to pay her bills and get money from a man instead of getting a job and go to work so she can take care of her children and stop being a free will for men to just come and live with you also with your children because she is not living to please god only to please man she is not a very clean person I have to say that she thought she was a clean individual but she only like to make her kids clean up and then when they clean up they don't wash they hands at all dig in their nose and go in the kitchen and cook food. And the mom only do what is best for her and not her children she only thinking about herself and her man ok I'm sorry that I stayed in her house at night I pray so can get me out of her house she don't clean up enough for me I glad that god has blessed me with the money sofa with the skin peeling off the inside era 7 it plus my mother would not want me living at her house she is a pig and am glad to be coming home thank you Jesus I was upset but god show me that not where he is taking me she has not hold down a job she only like milky nigger for money instead of getting a job and support her family but she don't know how to do that getting some self respect and not relying on men to give her money. Life has challenge but when you are down and out you found out who your real friend are so I'm glad that I want be mad or upset because she is not my friend anymore but I'm praying that we I get my lights back on that I will get a steady income I remember my mother when she was living she had a friend like that somebody who say yeah that's my friend but all the time she just want what she and don't care about if she is sick or doing alright I am praying that god send me a friend that can really be a good friend and we do things together and I will never forget Tonia she want ever have to be in my present again she has lost a friend that would be Rhonda Waller so if she read or buy this book one day she will say down she really hate me know I don't just don't want you as a my friend anymore god is able to above all you can ask him I stay at my home house for 9 days since my lights are out again but thank god. God sent some money to get the lights back on I'm so thankful for that god see me he never left me god give me strength from day to day I love my savior and he love me I only knew her for about 6 years but there is a saying when you are down and out don't have a friend in this world people don't love you they just be talking with you to hold a conversation and make their self look good ask the question you know that I'm there for you in other words they really say you are on your own I am not going to help you so when you get a real person that really care and they do something to help you out if your situation but I have learned people in general say one thing and do something totally different and you can't trust your on people because like to be part of nothing but talking about you and putting down I wish my mother was here to give me some good advice and someone I could trust other than god Tonia Wheeler was a friend to me for about maybe 6 years but we fell out because I had to stay with her for 9 days and she got attitude with me cause I want to stay at her house until I got my lights back on so me and my son could how to move around in the house be able to cook and I love watching TV my soaps like you're in the restless and days of live and let's make a deal the price is right it feel like know one care about little old me but god care this happening for a reason and a season so just praise god for the good and the bad pray for better days for me and my son that that love me so much he is the only help that I'm getting my family don't care whether I be outdoor sleeping under a bridge or a homeless shelter my god has supply my needs so I can get the lights back on. She can tell me anything going with she ask for advice on relationship, life situation, family, men we talk about every day or every other day she very cool down to earth person she funny but she not funny then me I love her crazy self love all my best friends the women I mostly like thick bbw slim skinny smart fun funny short honest respectfully loyal faithfully be yourself cute who like video games also sports who want something in life that have goals in life like to have fun all the time I been thought a lot in my life since being a baby don't like my dad at all if I seen my dad ever in the future ask him what made you want to do this to me we did not have any lights in the house for three months or gas to cook but god and pray I was bless with the money to get the lights and gas back on it was cold he pneumonia while we was in the cold I made by the grace of god I thoughts that I was not going to survive being in the dark and cold house but god is faithful and true so I have been in a struggle because I have been fighting for my disability check for three I'm praying for a breakthrough in my clam god has bless me in so many ways thank god I love god when I was young spending time with great-grandmother in South Carolina mostly in the summer I start paying attention to her hair very different then most women my great mother mom was India didn't know that until my mom say something to me about it. It very possibility half black half India from my great grandmother genius cause a lot of people say feel like a warm heater my mom told that that to me also women as well I decided to be a activists speak local elementary school and middle school my loving mother is going help with the public speaking about bipolar disorder and ADHA disorder seen being a adult very difficult with women telling this illness about me I will mostly explain to my future finance when the time is right hope she accept about the ADHA disorder and bi-polar one of my elementary teacher find out having ADHA also her daughter have it she told me one day in class I have a lot of one on one session with teachers explain different classroom assignments to be good student start going to regular ed classes in the 8th grade at Henry Turner middle school in Atlanta Georgia I had a favorite school bus driver was Ms. Jackson in elementary school she was pretty cool with me I am pretty cook in the kitchen learn from grandmother and best friend also learn my mom how to cook I knew a lot of teachers and students in school a lot of people going to ask multiple question on ADHA disorder while doing public speaking I be prepare for all question to help kids and adults also from parents that have children's with mental illness kid or adults it different way that can trigger mental disorder would say about five ways really depends on how bad on the illness as for me it's couple ways that can make me talk different tone of voice in person or over the phone I try not to let people getting on my nervous so much as a adults. As a young kid it trigger very often like every other day sometimes every day of the week I have multiples hidden talents that keep explore new ideas to better myself in life would say listening to music while work out improve my fitness most of my family was not that fit different side of my family had some type of cancer do not want to get cancer at all since being in high school start watching my weight and being more health been a chunky kid grandmother feed a lot of good food gain some weight on me I would say around 9th grade still little chunky then start losing weight on my own I play a lot of football in the street in my neighborhood and tackle football I was always getting tackle playing football in the front yard and back yard my mom told me one day you starting to be slim down she say not her fat chunky checks son anymore now my mom be calling sexy as well handsome every since having abs now I might eat a lot of food still have a six-pack it took a long time get muscles and having six packs. When this year came in I thought that it would be a little easier for me because I have been through so much and I don't really have any family or friends to help me in my adversity that I have been experiencing so I have been praying for better days so I can live the life god would have me live I understand that life can throw you some curve balls and change your mind also your attitude on life my son don't think that he needs to support me in any kind way I'm problem to him because I always need money for house hold items and food bills sometimes just to have some so I want be broke not bother him all the time for money I believe he is getting tired of me and don't want to give me anymore money he said that I need a job to support myself and pay my house hold trouble so I'm going to get me a job doing something that don't require me asking him or other people for help he is so mean and selfish to his own mother and he don't think I need anything I am just a old person with no life and life has not been the same since my mom died because she loved me know matter what I ask for or why I ask for it she even send him money for school when he started college in 2012 but my faith is in god not my son or my not so loving family that's not helping me out at all she I say don't have any family they are died to me and my spirit god will provide for his child and I love god. God will bless me abundantly that is my pray every day that live too another day when I get up every morning and see a beautiful day or a cloudy day or rain I know that life is not easy but sometimes you need a little help in what you are planning on doing with your life is order by heavenly father May 28, 2016 I don't think that I can or make it without god every day of my life I will praise god for the blessings that's is coming my way I hope one day that I will make my mother proud of me and god me getting a job working at Wendy or dollar tree sometimes I wonder why was I born in this world people are so not caring or thoughtful they are fake people only think of their self my new friend is lashanda she is heaven sent angel from god he know what I need and he supply all my needs my heavenly father and I love him know body like him he is a great god I'm going to get my blessing from god life has got me in all season waiting on god and me living for him being obedient to god my son think that I need a job so I want have to worry him for money or food or paying the bills and giving me money to put in my pockets so I want be broke. I love my son but is bipolar disorder and ADHA he does not any kind of medicine to help stay come I wish my mother was here to help me with him to stay on track with his mental issues people on crack should not have any kids or be as round infants that is my belief of people that can't handle being a parent or rising kids but I pray for his dad to get clean one day and other people that is addictive to street drugs this is my life and my name is Rhonda Denise Waller, Teontry Timirrio Waller is the writer and author of this book my son is person that don't understand what or things happened in your life for a reason and a season because of god how you are going to deal with it and what to do about the situation and to try fix the problem for it to get better for you and the situation turn around for you and my has curse me out because have ask him for money for food and bills but I prayed for god to set him free of the enemy attack on me he needs some time of herbal medicine to keep him come I love him very much I will keep praying for him and his bipolar disorder to get better my son is very aggressive and mean sometimes I believe that disease make you crazy don't let do your full duty when you know that when put something in your heart you should fill full your dreams and ambitious when you called to do in this life achieve all that's in your future don't let know body brake your spirit to be all that god has plan for you in your future life is too short.

www.ingramcontent.com/pod-product-compliance
Lightning Source LLC
LaVergne TN
LVHW011730060526
838200LV00051B/3117